The Line of Succession

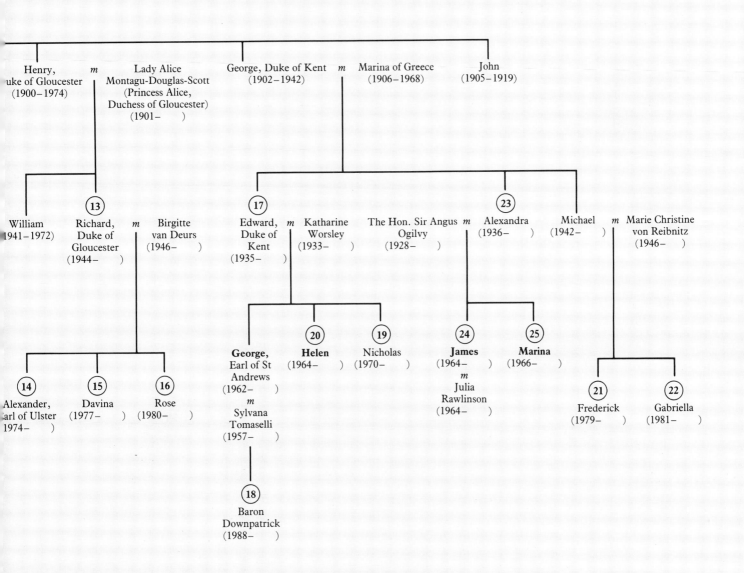

Henry,
Duke of Gloucester
(1900–1974)

m

Lady Alice
Montagu-Douglas-Scott
(Princess Alice,
Duchess of Gloucester)
(1901–   )

George, Duke of Kent
(1902–1942)

m

Marina of Greece
(1906–1968)

John
(1905–1919)

William
(1941–1972)

13 Richard,
Duke of
Gloucester
(1944–   )

m

Birgitte
van Deurs
(1946–   )

17 Edward,
Duke of
Kent
(1935–   )

m

Katharine
Worsley
(1933–   )

The Hon. Sir Angus
Ogilvy
(1928–   )

m

23 Alexandra
(1936–   )

Michael
(1942–   )

m

Marie Christine
von Reibnitz
(1946–   )

14 Alexander,
Earl of Ulster
(1974–   )

15 Davina
(1977–   )

16 Rose
(1980–   )

George,
Earl of St
Andrews
(1962–   )

m

Sylvana
Tomaselli
(1957–   )

20 **Helen**
(1964–   )

19 Nicholas
(1970–   )

24 **James**
(1964–   )

m

Julia
Rawlinson
(1964–   )

25 **Marina**
(1966–   )

21 Frederick
(1979–   )

22 Gabriella
(1981–   )

18 Baron
Downpatrick
(1988–   )

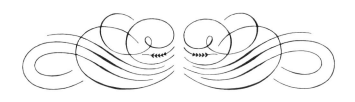

'My young friends...'

The Queen's Young Family

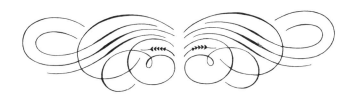

Valerie Garner and Jayne Fincher

WEIDENFELD AND NICOLSON
London

Acknowledgments

Jayne Fincher and I would like to thank everyone who – on or off the record – helped in the research for this book.

We are especially grateful to His Royal Highness The Prince Edward for allowing us to use the specially commissioned photographs of himself taken at Windsor Castle.

Our thanks are due also to Viscount Linley and his team at David Linley Ltd, The Lady Elizabeth Anson, John Haslam, Mona Mitchell, Norman Adams, RA, and Laura Scott of the Royal Academy School, Ann Wallace and Adrian Vincent.

We are especially grateful to our colleague Christopher Warwick for his generous help, and thanks also to Douglas Keay for allowing me to quote from his work, and to Doreen Montgomery for her guidance.

VALERIE GARNER

FOR OUR HUSBANDS: J.L.G. AND A.R.B.

Copyright: Text © Valerie Garner 1989
Photographs © Jayne Fincher 1989

Published in Great Britain by
George Weidenfeld & Nicolson Limited
91 Clapham High Street
London SW4 7TA

Designed by Gaye Allen

ISBN 0 297 79518

Printed in Great Britain by
Butler & Tanner Ltd
Frome and London

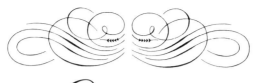

Contents

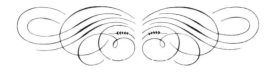

Prince Edward's weekday working life back-stage in London's Palace Theatre is very different to the life he leads at weekends.

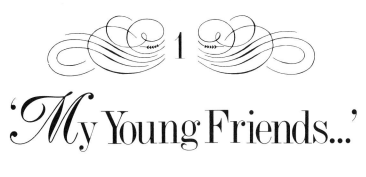

1

'My Young Friends...'

When Prince Edward, the Queen's youngest son, originally destined for a conventional royal career in the services, found himself a job as Production Assistant of The Really Useful Theatre Company, it was assumed there had been some dramatic scenes backstage at Buckingham Palace.

Household theatricals have been part of royal entertainment for centuries. Queen Victoria liked them so much she had a stage built with sumptuous red velvet curtains in the Waterloo Room at Windsor Castle. But for the monarch's son actually to work for a theatre company and be paid a salary would, even five years ago, have created an appreciable *frisson* at court.

The Queen and the Duke of Edinburgh surprised everyone by taking the news calmly and with evident pleasure. 'You won't believe it – they are both thrilled,' Edward told a relative who had inquired with some interest about their reaction. The Prince was clearly delighted and relieved by the enthusiasm with which his parents greeted the news of this unlikely choice of career for a member of the Royal Family so close to the throne.

It certainly took some careful thought on the part of the Queen and the Duke. But Edward's path had, to some extent, been smoothed by his sister-in-law the Duchess of York, and his first cousin Viscount Linley, son of Princess Margaret and Lord Snowdon, who both have commercial jobs. They have been the successful working examples that have stimulated a significant change of attitude on the future employment of royal siblings as their proximity to the throne lessens with the arrival of each child of the Prince and Princess of Wales. But it could not have been an easy decision for the Queen and her husband as it was shadowed by concern that close members of their family circle involved in commercial enterprises of any kind could, however indirectly, leave the monarchy vulnerable to embarrassment or scandal.

Sir Angus Ogilvy, husband of Princess Alexandra, experienced some of the problems when he resigned from the board of Lonrho, an international mining and finance group, which later came under fire in a Department of Trade report. At the time he had many directorships, all of which he relinquished because of his royal connections. It is known he now feels that personal or business problems are a handicap to anyone within the royal circle – although he considers his own two children, James and Marina, are far enough removed from the throne to be concerned.

But there are six other lively young men and women who could be affected by the careful but out-dated philistinism which has decreed, in the past, that suitable careers for young royals lie in the services and other non-commercial fields.

Apart from the Duchess of York, who was a commoner, they are all royally born; descended from over a thousand years of Kings, Emperors and Tsars. But that is no reason to spend the rest of their lives in an outdated royal rut furrowed by their predecessors in the Windsor dynasty.

At one time the only future for those members of the family not actively engaged in the business of being royal, was in the services or in governing some outpost of the now vanished Empire. The women were not expected to have jobs, although anything remotely artistic was acceptable – but only as a hobby.

As the Queen's family expands vigorously and the number of lead players increases there is little need for less senior royals who helped out when the Queen was young. As her generation emerged there were few younger members of the family available. When she was old enough Princess Alexandra of Kent was brought in to help and she has been a valued member of the team ever since, although far down the line of seniority.

So the go-ahead was given for exemption from the system for those of the latest grown-up generation whose places in the succession are down the line. Now they are turning up all over the place in a variety of jobs and their stories of life in their working worlds are said to keep the Queen vastly entertained.

When she says, 'My young friends have been telling me ...' and launches into one of her perceptive, amusing anecdotes, the chances are it stems from one of her close family who is leading a workaday life that would have been unthinkable in previous decades.

'I'm in feelthy commerce,' says David Linley, grinning widely as he stresses the vowel. It is clear he revels in the commercial success of his job as the first royal carpenter.

Viscount Linley, twenty-seven, grandson of King George VI and Queen Elizabeth the Queen Mother, and nephew of Queen Elizabeth II, is happiest with the feel of wood beneath his hands, earning his living in one of the oldest crafts known to man.

'Things are different now and we are actually doing what we want to do,' he replies in his quiet, understated way to questions, often from Americans eager to buy his wares, who are fascinated to know why Princess Margaret's son is a 'chippy'. But David, as he likes everyone to call him, is well aware that should he, at any time, have the misfortune to walk a financial tightrope with his furniture-making business or part-share in a restaurant, the rumblings from Buckingham and Kensington Palaces would be formidable.

In the competitive hurly-burly outside the protective atmosphere of the palaces in which most of the young royals grew up, it is not always helpful to have the Queen as mother-in-law, parent, aunt or cousin. But they are successfully proving it is no longer the major handicap to living a normal working life it may once have been. 'Perhaps it even helps a little at first,' David Linley concedes. 'But later – well, they won't buy the furniture if it is no good.'

Looking at the careers of his sister-in-law, younger brother and cousins, the Prince of Wales must sometimes wish it were possible to have a fulfilling personal job outside the stylized boundaries inevitably predestined for the heir to the throne. In the next decade, standing at the crossroads between one century and another, Charles will have much to say about how the monarchy is steered into the uncertain future and how each member of the Royal Family can best adapt to changing times. He is only too aware that, as Sir Roy Strong, former Curator of the Victoria and Albert Museum, once put it, 'Abuse of the Monarchy can erode it.'

The arrival of the Queen's fifth grandchild highlighted the type of media hysteria which

Viscount Linley and his sister, Lady Sarah Armstrong-Jones, are an integral part of the Royal Family, although they live liberated workaday lives with very different life-styles.

Charles and Diana are pictured at their home, Highgrove, in Gloucestershire, in a study taken to celebrate the Prince's fortieth birthday.

could do just that. As *The Sunday Times* so sensibly said in retrospect about the event, 'A thriving 6 pounds, 12 ounces baby girl was born to a healthy, 28-year-old woman in a London hospital last Tuesday.'

Every other newspaper, except the *Independent* which disdainfully gave the birth ten words on page two, thrilled, gushed and crooned over Sarah York's baby. The Duke of Edinburgh, like the majority of men in the land, was said to be totally nonplussed and exasperated by the unprecedented 'hype' surrounding the arrival of the first princess of the new generation.

Prince Andrew acted decisively to quell the commotion. He whisked his women away to the comparative peace of Balmoral without even going home to Castlewood House first. 'He wanted to start family life quietly,' said an aide.

The problem the Royal Family has to face in the future is how far can it go without erosion eating away the framework and fabric of the monarchy itself? Upon Prince Charles and his heir falls the responsibility of either preserving the *status quo* or shaping it into a compatible sovereignty more in accord with the twenty-first century. Backing him will be a – hopefully – strong family circle; the inner ring composed of his two brothers and sister and their families; the outer band consisting of the Gloucester, Kent, Snowdon and Ogilvy cousins; all with an amalgam of talents.

11

Any monarch, however down-to-earth, is inevitably somewhat removed from everyday life by factors like security which tend to dominate freedom of movement. And the maintenance of that quality of aloofness is deemed essential if the much-quoted, so-called 'mystique' is to be preserved.

Trapped in this regal lazaretto it is all the more important to have a string of cousins living ordinary lives which can brush off beneficially on the Sovereign, forever inhibited by a circumstance of birth.

Elizabeth Longford has pointed out how important she believes 'the cousinship' to be. In *Elizabeth II* she writes, 'An essential factor for a flourishing Royal Family – plenty of blood relations but all fanning out and connecting with different walks of life . . .'

The younger members of the family are touchy about being quoted on anything that is remotely connected with their relative the Queen. But one of them said, 'I am everlastingly grateful that I was not born further up the line; that I am on the flip-side of the family and can go out and do a normal job of work.'

It was an impromptu, off-the-cuff remark but it summed up the feelings of the younger royals who have broken the Palace mould of past generations. With the Queen's support and encouragement they are shaking free of the strict rules that have shackled all close family links with 'Her upstairs', as staff sometimes irreverently refer to their royal mistress.

As he likes service life the Duke of York, the Queen's second son, is following a traditional path for the foreseeable future, prepared to conform to an accepted pattern by upholding his family's customary role in the Royal Navy. But his restless, talented wife, the former Sarah Ferguson, needs an outlet for her energies outside her function as senior royal Duchess and has convinced both the Queen and her husband that she should continue her career in publishing.

The Duchess of York enjoyed canoeing during a visit to Canada in 1987.

Nevertheless, after some tactful advice she has carefully cut her ties with any one firm and is working as a freelance from the Yorks' temporary home Castlewood House, loaned by King Hussein of Jordan. Friends say she finds it therapeutic to have a responsible job that is so different from the royal one and – apart from any other consideration – as a Navy wife, any money she earns is useful.

The most experienced working girl in the family, Sarah has always earned her living and has no intention of giving it up. When she became engaged to Andrew she made it clear that her intention was to go on with her career after marriage, and even motherhood has not changed her mind. 'I am still very firm about working and quite determined not to allow public duties to crowd out my schedule,' was her reaction when asked if she might now have little time for a career outside her job as Duchess of York.

She has a vast network of friends from walks of life not always known to royalty: rock stars, designers, tycoons, television personalities. Many others from the international set have been introduced into the circle of royal cousins and have broadened it considerably. As the most worldly and experienced of them, Sarah is the archetype for her young relatives-by-marriage and they all react to her drive and energy. Most of them have benefited from her good-natured optimism, including brother-in-law Edward when he made the decision to quit the Royal Marines. It was a move which understandably upset his parents but, amid all the furore, Sarah sensibly set about researching among her friends to find a job Edward would like. But eventually he found it for himself from Andrew Lloyd-Webber, the composer and impressario – one of his own contacts within the theatrical world he so loves.

Even now, grown up and, in most cases, living totally uninhibited lives the younger members of 'the cousinship' are wary of intrusion into that other protocol-bordered world in which they occasionally appear. Invitations to most great affairs of State and functions where the Royal Family show a united front are usually automatic. Except for Sarah York they have all spent most Christmas holidays with the Queen since they were born and see a side of her glimpsed only by her most intimate family circle.

Talking to them there is one unmentionable topic – 'The Family', which just happens to be royal. A curiously familiar look comes over each young face as if the shutters have come down. It is a taboo subject that is the swiftest way to end a conversation with any of the demi-royals. Like the good manners their nannies taught them, the observance of silence on all family matters has been instilled into every member of the Royal Family since childhood and no relaxed style of living will eradicate it.

'They all still retain just a touch of royalness,' observed Lady Elizabeth Anson, the Queen's cousin who has watched them all grow up – with the exception of the Duchess of York.

Somehow, even in the informal way in which most of them live, the barriers never quite come down and royal privacy remains steadfastly protected.

The Queen looks on them all as her extended family, gathers them round her for major celebrations and loves to hear all their news. She is becoming quite knowledgeable about aspects of life that normally never cross her path. As an extremely protected youngster herself she never had the opportunity to mix with ordinary people like her own children have done. 'Remember I did not go to school,' she gently reminded Princess Anne's headmistress who had been trying to explain a facet of school life.

So the adventures – doubtless carefully edited – of the cousins are a source of interest and amusement to a woman who has never really been beyond 'the glass curtain', as her old governess, the late Marion Crawford, once described the barrier between the Queen's world and that of her subjects.

Viscount Linley and his sister Lady Sarah Armstrong-Jones, twenty-five, grew up

Lady Sarah Armstrong-Jones hates the limelight and avoids photographers. She faces the cameras rarely, usually to support her brother at one of his business parties.

Lady Helen Windsor likes parties and London's high-life. But she is also ambitious to build a career in the art world.

behind that curtain. But they had the good fortune to have a father, Lord Snowdon, who was very much of the real world and wanted it for his children. Princess Margaret did not allow the unhappiness of their subsequent divorce to affect joint decisions about their children's future. She has always championed the emergence of young royals – or, more correctly, demi-royals in the case of David and Sarah – into a more cosmopolitan world than she knew before her marriage. They have grown up in a circle of their parents' friends – artists, show-biz people and media colleagues – and were always encouraged in artistic pursuits. 'I first learnt about carpentry and design in my father's work-room,' said David.

His sister, a great favourite of the Queen and the Princess of Wales, is quiet and rather shy. She is rarely without her sketch book and is determined to be a serious artist. Sarah has already had examples of her work hung in the Royal Academy's Summer Exhibitions and, if she continues to be successful, may well find her paintings and drawings sold by her cousin and close friend Lady Helen Windsor.

Helen, daughter of the Duke and Duchess of Kent, is a blonde, bouncy extrovert who works as an assistant in a fine arts gallery in London. Born three days before Sarah she, too, is a seriously hard worker in her job despite her playgirl image in the gossip columns.

Her elder brother George, the Earl of St Andrews, twenty-seven, heir to the Dukedom of Kent, is a budding diplomat whose first job for the Foreign Office was as Third Secretary in the British Embassy in politically sensitive Budapest.

He and his clever Canadian wife, Sylvana – currently working on a book on France and Scotland in the eighteenth century – spent the final part of their honeymoon travelling by car to Hungary after a controversial registry office wedding. Neither the Queen nor the Duke of Edinburgh, his godfather, could attend as the bride was both Roman Catholic and divorced. George was accordingly eliminated from his place in the succession but as he was number eighteen at that time, it scarcely mattered.

Princess Alexandra's son, James Ogilvy, twenty-five (but he was a Leap Year baby and only has an official birthday every four years), is now working as a City investment trainee and was the first royal to sign on at a job centre. He has also founded a magazine, served in a guards regiment and worked as a navvy in a bottle-making factory. He was interested in a career in journalism but his father, former City businessman Angus Ogilvy, felt it would be wiser for him to have some business training. James married beautiful Julia Rawlinson in July 1988, and most of the Royal Family were at his Essex wedding.

His younger sister Marina, bubbly and curly haired is the most adventurous of the royal cousins. In 1985 at the age of nineteen, she won a place on Operation Raleigh, the round-the-world adventure expedition for young people. 'It was the biggest challenge of her life,' said one of her close friends. During her three months away Marina swam in crocodile-infested waters, was plagued by leeches and helped in a project to build hospitals in Belize, Central America.

When she returned she worked as an £80-a-week instructor teaching inner city youngsters – who had no idea who she was – how to survive in the rugged countryside of north-west Scotland. She is now completing a domestic science course which she hopes will help in her aim to devote her working life to youngsters not so fortunate as herself.

All the young working royals are artistic and it comes as no surprise to older members

James Ogilvy married beautiful Julia Rawlinson in July 1988, and most of the Royal Family were at his Saffron Walden wedding.

Marina Ogilvy is more often seen in rugged clothes on Outward Bound expeditions. But here she is in conventional gear for a family wedding.

David Linley revels in the commercial success of his job as the first royal carpenter. 'Things are different now and we are doing what we want to do,' he says.

of the family who feel that these talents have come down through the regal genes from Queen Victoria. Her personal legacy included the solid Victorian family values – the virtues Margaret Thatcher praises so much – upon which the young royals were raised.

But Victoria bequeathed something more to her great-great-great-grandchildren – Edward, David, Sarah, Helen, George, James and Marina – a love of the creative arts. The Victorian hobbies of writing, acting, painting, designing and carving wood are now being channelled into full-time careers in commercial enterprises which would, doubtless, have horrified the old Queen.

But how Princess Marie-Louise, one of King George V's cousins and herself a talented artist, would have envied them their opportunities. When she had to ask the King's permission to travel on a bus he said anxiously, 'I wonder what Grandmama would have thought.' As if the Queen's ghost was about to rap him on the knuckles.

King George III, more usually remembered for his treatment of the American colonies and an illness believed to be porphyria which caused him to have bouts of 'madness', was an artistic and cultivated monarch who has been hotly championed by the Prince of Wales. All the younger royals except the Duchess of York are directly descended from him and surely this King was the regal common denominator of all their talents.

He was an accomplished artist who founded the Royal Academy of Arts and its associated school where Lady Sarah Armstrong-Jones now studies; he was a writer – many of his essays on Whig history are in the archives at Windsor – and he had a passion for the theatre, producing his own plays at the Castle and acting in them when he was young.

His great interest in books inspired the foundation of the British Library in the British Museum. Furniture was another consuming interest and he was extremely knowledgeable about it, particularly on the work of Chippendale and William Vile, which he collected. Research does not show, however, that he actually tried his hand at furniture-making as his descendant David Linley has done so successfully. Queen Victoria's sons did, however. They had a carpentry 'shop' at Osborne, and their tools were inscribed with their names.

George III also built up the royal art collection, including the priceless Canalettos, and had his whole family painted by Gainsborough – the famous collection that King George VI hung in the Long Gallery at Windsor as the artist had originally intended.

The difference between the past and the present is that then members of the Royal Family patronized the arts; now they are participating.

But if George III was the fount of varied talents for his descendants he can also be found accountable for the Royal Marriages Act of 1772, which can sometimes be inconvenient. So it has proved for Prince Michael of Kent and, some years later, for his nephew the Earl of St Andrews when they both wished to marry Roman Catholic divorcees. Each had to forfeit his place in the Succession although it can pass to their children.

The Act was formulated to prevent unacceptable marriages by George III's large family of fifteen sons and daughters. But it is still very much in force as Princess Margaret found when she wanted to marry Group Captain Peter Townsend in the Fifties.

No matter how forcibly the Queen's young relatives may argue they are not royal, they are in the line of succession and, technically, bound by the Act.

At the birth of Prince William, Buckingham Palace drew up an official list of twenty-three names within the Royal Family. This has now been increased by three with the births of Prince Harry, Princess Beatrice of York and Baron Downpatrick. Nothing short of a catastrophic tragedy would see most of the names on the list anywhere near the throne. But, for instance, it the Princess of Wales insists on her children travelling with herself and Prince Charles, and any misfortune occurred there could be three names off the top of the list simultaneously, leaving the York dynasty as heirs to the throne, as it has been for the last two reigns.

The Duke and Duchess show their new baby, Beatrice, to the waiting crowds outside London's Portland Hospital.

A Whole Lotta Woman

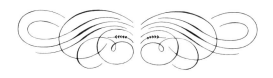

It is not easy to be part of the Queen's intimate family circle and not be influenced by her deep commitment to the duty she swore to perform when, still a young wife and mother, she became Sovereign two months before her twenty-sixth birthday.

It was the age of Sarah Ferguson when she joined the Royal Family on 23 July 1986. Since that summer day when she became Duchess of York the subtle guiding influence of her mother-in-law has gently bridled some of the spontaneous exuberance but none of the spirit and mettle that make her such a character.

Sarah has steadied down considerably since her marriage and the birth of her baby but she is still the sparkling young woman with whom the Queen's second son fell in love. Now she has a real stake in the family firm – a princess who is currently fifth in line to the throne, after her father and young cousins.

This royal baby, born in the happiest of circumstances to parents so clearly devoted, is certain to play a major role in the Royal Family in the next century. Born on the luckiest day of the waning century, 8.8.88 at 8.18 pm, the York baby has the additional good fortune to have a mother who has resolutely kept the common touch.

'Fergie', the name she and Andrew hate, but by which she will always affectionately be called, has even made her husband behave like a normal, happy human being – something royal princes find difficult in public. She has brought warmth and love into his life along with an abundance of fun and laughter and an end to loneliness.

But it has not always been easy. The Duchess of York is an independent woman who likes her own way. Indeed some of the more experienced royal observers are sceptical, even now, that an emancipated working girl of twenty-nine can be successfully transplanted into the very heart of a jealously guarded 'magic circle'.

Jaunty, fizzy, sexy Fergie with a curvaceous figure of which her husband's great-great-grandfather, King Edward VII, would have approved, is still a typical product of 'the jolly-hockey-sticks brigade'.

'Never change,' said her father, Major Ronald Ferguson, on her wedding day. It seems unlikely she ever will completely conform to the accepted pattern of a Royal Duchess – particularly the senior one.

The others are older, of course, and were firmly trained by their mothers-in-law, the Dowager Duchesses who, in their turn, had been rigidly taught protocol and restraint by

The Duke and Duchess of York, just back from honeymoon, join the Queen and the Prince and Princess of Wales to celebrate the Queen Mother's birthday in August 1986.

their mother-in-law that formidable matriarch, Queen Mary, Consort of King George V.

Birgitte of Gloucester and Katharine of Kent, who were both commoners, have emerged as carefully elegant, dignified royal ladies who each make a substantial contribution to the success of the British monarchy. But Sarah York is from a new generation and has her own very different royal style. She finds it difficult to be anything but totally natural and some of her unaffected joyous outlook is beginning to brush off on the rest of the family.

The Queen who normally puts on her 'Miss Piggy' face – tight-lipped and stern – when she is really full of happiness and love, laughed with delight on a public engagement the day after her fifth grandchild was born. In a way it was a tribute to her uninhibited daughter-in-law and showed they were having the right kind of influence on each other.

Sarah travelled an unusually roundabout route for a royal bride, via two well-publicized love affairs which, in the past, might have affected the chances of a happy outcome to her romance with such a close family member of the House of Windsor. But the Queen, showing great understanding towards a much-loved second son, looked beyond the past loves of Sarah Ferguson to the contribution she might make in the future as Andrew's wife.

Sarah was no stranger to the Royal Family. The Queen and the Duke of Edinburgh had known the younger daughter of his polo manager since she had first toddled on to Smith's Lawn, Windsor, to watch her father play.

Jaunty, fizzy, sexy Fergie is still a typical product of the 'jolly hockey-sticks' brigade. The 'It's a Knockout' charity tournament, masterminded by brother-in-law Prince Edward, saw her behaving in typical rumbustious style.

Sarah Margaret, second child of Susan and Ronald Ferguson, was born a few minutes after 9 am on the autumn morning of 15 October 1959, in a nursing home not far from the one in which her own daughter was born nearly twenty-nine years later.

As the red-haired infant, who would one day be known the world over simply as 'Fergie', appeared in the world, her future mother-in-law, the Queen, was five months' pregnant with her third child Prince Andrew. But their linked destiny, which was to make such a lively and distinctive contribution to the Royal Family, was still in the unknown future. Their first encounter came when, like all the children of polo players, they went to watch their fathers play.

Sarah's mother, now Mrs Hector Barrantes, says the youngsters met 'behind the pony lines', and also in the gardens of Windsor Castle where the Ferguson girls, as children of the Life Guards officer who became Commander of the Sovereign's Escort, were allowed to play.

Later, as a schoolgirl with the fiery hair and colouring of her Celtic ancestry, Sarah met Andrew again. They were among a small gang of children who played behind the pony lines, galloping around and emulating their elders in the field.

There was one sparky incident when Andrew called tomboy Sarah 'Carrots' and she retaliated with a spirited attack which left him laughing helplessly. Now he adores his wife's

Above: *Bare feet were the easiest way to land ashore after a flying leap from the boat in which Sarah and Andrew visited Trou aux Biches in October 1987.* Left: *Sarah's natural, uninhibited style was a great hit with the locals as she waved a Mauritian flag during a walk-about in Quatre Cocos, October 1987.*

beautiful hair which he describes as 'Titian' and begs her not to cut it short.

Sarah grew up voluble, outspoken and, above all, terrific fun. She is a natural communicator and has even begun to tame her husband's relations with the media – although like all 'born royals' he'll never be totally convinced that the 'rat-pack' can be trusted. Nevertheless he managed a previously unheard of few words of thanks to photographers and reporters who had covered their highly successful Canadian tour.

After their baby was born, Sarah, safely tucked away in her exclusive private room far from the surging crowds of press and public outside the Portland Hospital, urged him to go out for a chat. Smiling happily, he did, 'just like any other proud father,' as one newspaper put it, which made the weary hours of waiting in the rare August heat worthwhile.

Sarah herself did let her cordial relations with Fleet Street and Wapping deteriorate perceptibly earlier in the summer after her father was alleged to have been found visiting a Wigmore Street massage parlour of doubtful repute. She scowled ferociously at photographers and, on one of her appearances after the disclosures, shook her long hair over her face so they would get no decent pictures.

But Fergie didn't stay angry for long. She has the quality of always understanding other points of view and appreciated that, savage as the attack on her father had been, everyone concerned was doing a job – however unsavoury.

Above: *Sarah met her mother, Mrs Susan Barrantes, in New York in January 1988, and told her of her pregnancy. Whilst there, she attended the US première of* Phantom of the Opera, *and afterwards met up with Prince Edward's boss, Andrew Lloyd-Webber, and his wife, Sarah Brightman, and Michael Crawford, stars of the show.*

The Duke of York took flowers to his Duchess after the birth of their daughter. He beamed and chatted to the crowds outside the Portland Hospital and took their good wishes to his wife.

Right: *Sarah and her father, Major Ronald Ferguson, shortly before the 'massage parlour' scandal broke. They are at a polo match in Palm Springs, USA.*

Someone at Buckingham Palace once said, 'If the Queen is on your side – you don't need anyone else.' This Sarah found during the storm over 'that massage parlour business', as it was referred to by an official of the court.

There were those in the royal circle not entirely surprised by the allegations, but most were appalled at the effect the undoubted scandal, whether true or not, might have on the pregnant Duchess – not to mention her stepmother, Susan, of whom she was very fond.

News of Sarah's pregnancy had been known to a few in the Royal Family since Christmas 1987. But it was not until she had told her mother when they met in New York the following month that the news was released.

It was while Sarah was in New York on a public engagement, that she had the kind of experience the Royal Family dread after the assassination of Earl Mountbatten. An IRA supporter lunged at her with a six-foot flag pole shouting 'Murderer, murderer'. Sarah, only a few weeks pregnant and at the dangerous stage for a miscarriage, was shaken. But unflappable as ever, she shrugged off the incident.

Back home on 25 January she celebrated the official announcement of her pregnancy by flying her helicopter over her old home at Dummer where Susan Ferguson and her children had put out a large sheet inscribed with the words, 'Congrats, Ma'am.' It made Sarah smile high above them.

She wasn't smiling, however, on the Sunday morning some time later when a tabloid broke the story that her father had been frequenting a massage parlour in Wigmore Street for reasons which, when disclosed, certainly embarrassed the Royal Family and hurt his own.

Photographers waited two days in a van outside the club to get their pictures of him leaving. It was an unedifying piece of journalism which left a considerable dent in Sarah's pride – and faith. She defended the Major staunchly by actions rather than words, giving him a daughterly 'thumbs up' when she saw him at the Royal Windsor Horse Show days later.

The unfortunate man had to ride out the storm which came at a particularly difficult and busy time for him with the polo season in full swing and frequent meetings with royals already scheduled.

The Queen must have found it all highly embarrassing and the mother in her was naturally worried about Sarah and her unborn child. She decided to visit Balmoral for the week-end where Andrew had taken his wife to get away from the 'flack' which was upsetting her considerably.

In the peace of the Aberdeenshire hills the Queen spoke gently and compassionately to the young woman who was carrying her latest grandchild. Sarah, though creditably loyal to her father, was desperately upset and took some reassuring, but the effects of the Queen's visit restored her aplomb and confidence.

Her Majesty's piercing Windsor blue eyes can harden to glacial depths when offended but she can readily forgive. A public pardon for whatever Major Ferguson may or may not have done was the easiest way out of the mess – and this Sarah asked of her mother-in-law, according to a friend. It was graciously given with a smile and a handshake the next time the Queen saw him, which was during an expected visit to Smith's Lawn for a polo occasion.

Some members of the family, however, were not so sympathetic towards the Major. It was felt, most strongly, that he had put the Queen in an intolerable position. Some were of the opinion that he should have resigned immediately both as Polo Manager to the Prince of Wales and as Deputy Chairman of the Guard's Polo Club, which, as it turned out, he did leave some months later.

Prince Charles himself appears to have reacted in a typically steadfast and loyal way. He intensely dislikes 'character assassination' by the media, and stoutly supported the Major through the worst of his ordeal. At the height of the publicity, as is the usual form, the Royal Family closed ranks around Sarah, its newest member. Smiling, the Queen Mother walked with Sarah to the paddock at Ascot, graciously sharing the affectionate warmth of the crowds. And there was genuine approval in the applause from the packed ranks of race-goers – most of them women – for the mettle of the heavily pregnant Duchess in braving the crowds when she could easily have remained in the sanctuary of the Royal Box.

Andrew could not be present to support his wife as, by that time, he had sailed with his ship HMS *Edinburgh* on the long sea voyage to Australia. But the Queen took particular care to surround her second – and some say favourite – daughter-in-law with those she loved: her mother Mrs Susan Barrantes and her maternal grandmother the Hon. Mrs Doreen Wright, eighty four, rode with Sarah in the open landau to the meeting. And her Argentinian-born step-father Hector Barrantes, still at that time banned from playing polo in Britain because of the Falklands conflict, was a guest in the Royal Box.

It was a perfect example of family solidarity and a typically royal attitude to a disagreeable scandal. An 'if we don't look, it will go away' approach the Queen has tried before with great success. Sarah was surrounded by a determinedly happy family party at Ascot that afternoon augmented by the good will so apparent in the crowds below.

The heavily pregnant Duchess of York walks with the Queen Mother to the paddock at Ascot Races.

Andrew aboard his ship HMS Edinburgh *on the long voyage to Australia where she took part in the Bi-centennial celebrations.*

Left: *Waiting for Beatrice: for such an energetic person the lull which the final month of pregnancy brought into Sarah's life, was tedious.*

Right: *Flying lessons were one of the Duchess's wedding presents. Here she is at RAF Scampton in May 1987.*

In the weeks before he left, Andrew had given her 'loving support', according to a Ferguson family friend who added, 'He was extremely sensitive and protective over the affair.' If anything it strengthened the deeply passionate relationship that ignites the Yorks. They are both intensely physical people and, fired by their love, share a powerful happiness upon which the Queen beams approvingly.

When they are parted they speak to each other every day, even from the other side of the world. During the last weeks of her pregnancy there was a satellite call booked every day. Sarah left the Royal Box at Wimbledon to receive one such call in the crowded All England Club's main office. Andrew was relaxing beside a swimming pool in Malta. 'Don't tell me about it – I don't want to hear about the wonderful sunshine,' Sarah told him. Later she went along to the women's dressing room where she sat and chatted to the players. 'He phones me to see how I am; what I've been doing. I told him the baby seems fine. I hate to think what it costs,' she said.

Sarah's normally hectic life became suddenly very quiet towards the end of her pregnancy. No flying, no four-in-hand carriage-driving, no riding – on the firm orders of her obstetrician Anthony Kenney.

Sarah filled in some of her spare time by transferring her love of helicopters – which, incidently the Queen hates – to writing about them for children. She tried out the stories about a helicopter called 'Budgie' on her half-brother and sisters, Andrew, Alice and Eliza, and on Princes William and Harry, who loved them. It seemed a perfect project with which to enliven her months of waiting and maybe a new twist to her publishing career.

Helicopters have been a passion with Sarah since she met Andrew. She even asked for choppers and teddy bears to be incorporated somewhere in the design of her wedding dress – an idea which designer Linda Cierach did not however include in the finished gown.

She loves teddy bears devotedly and a large toy accompanied the newly married pair in the honeymoon landau. When her new puppy 'Bendicks' – after her favourite chocolates – went on a first outing in Sarah's car he was snugly tucked up beside her teddy bear.

After the birth of Sarah's baby, flower replicas of teddy bears arrived as unusual bouquets from friends like the Prime Minister and Denis Thatcher who obviously knew of her liking for them. And when she left hospital a teddy bear badge announcing 'I'm a mum' was proudly worn on her dress – a present from Prince William.

Helicopters also have become an integral part of the Duchess's life, and one of the many perks of being a royal was the wedding gift of flying lessons, which she joyfully accepted so that she'd be able to share Andrew's life even more.

Sarah passed her fixed wing pilot's licence test in February 1987, and then took helicopter lessons which Air Hanson gave her as an £8,000 wedding present. Sarah flew solo in just forty-one hours, which impressed Andrew as he'd taken eighty-five hours to get his military helicopter wings.

She progressed to rotary blades in a Jet Ranger at RAF Benson under two instructors, Captain Kevin Mulhearn and Tim Kyle, ex-navy pilots employed by Air Hanson. Sarah also joined the Tiger Flying Club where she can fly Tiger Moths.

'I just want to understand his [Andrew's] job and know what he is talking about,' she said. But the most exciting moment of her flying career must have been when she looped the loop with the Red Arrows.

Sarah visited the formation team at RAF Scampton with Andrew. 'Take care of her,' he said, as, dressed in khaki overalls, she went up in a Bulldog aircraft with Squadron Leader David Walby who taught Prince Andrew and Prince Edward to fly.

With him, high over the River Humber, the Duchess took the controls and looped the loop. 'I've done it,' she cried in typical Sarah fashion. The Squadron Leader obviously admired her performance. 'Great courage and nerve,' he said later.

She needed both when Andrew took her paddling in canoes on a primitive adventure into the wilds of Canada along the Thelon River. Over her face was a net to protect her from the infamous blackflies; tucked into a corner of her ruck-sack was some Japanese moisturising cream made of silk which she hoped would protect her face with its delicate, fine freckled skin.

Caribou Rapids was chosen as the start of the canoe trip which took them three hundred miles into the North-West Territory. Andrew had wanted Sarah – whom the Canadians called 'Fergie Crockett' – to see the wild country he had first loved as a schoolboy in Canada.

On her canoe, which she shared with an experienced canoeist, expedition leader David Thompson, was the motto 'Never underestimate the power of this woman.' All those on the trip with them were agreed that this suited Sarah perfectly. She had started the tour, reckoned one of the most successful by a member of the Royal Family in Canada in recent years, with a decided disadvantage.

Some of the Canadian media were averse to their visit and greeted them rudely, calling Sarah 'Big Red'. The *Toronto Sun* even went as far as saying, 'What a lot of fuss over a guy who once dated a porn actress, and a giggly disco queen who made the headlines by poking a gent in the bum with an umbrella at Ascot.'

This was a reference to a shared, high-spirited and entirely harmless escapade with Diana that had earned some criticism. It would have gone unnoticed except by the friend for whom it was intended, but a watchful photographer got himself a classic picture of the royal sisters-in-law at play.

Princesses and Duchesses have to be alert to such things and it was yet another lesson for them both. But Sarah was catching on fast, as she proved on the Canadian trip which ended in praise for a job well done.

The Duchess of York may go all out to sell Britain abroad, as she did when they visited

Sarah York has her own very individual royal style. Extrovert and showy, she loved the effect of this cow-girl outfit, complete with stetson and green fringed suede jacket worn at a rodeo at Medicine Hat in 1987.

Below: *The Duke and Duchess of York, so obviously very much in love, visit the favourite honeymoon resort of Niagara Falls during their Canadian visit. Sarah has brought warmth and love into Andrew's life, along with an abundance of fun and laughter, and an end to loneliness.*

Above: *'I don't know how I'm going to survive ten days of black-flies,' said the Duchess of York as she prepared for a canoe expedition 'splash-off' in Canada, July 1987.*

Fergie's often misguided taste in clothes, is now legendary. Here she 'gilds the lily' with silk flowers and small birds in her hair at a fashion show in Los Angeles, USA.

This is better. The Duchess of York looking her best in a low-cut black cocktail dress at the Queensway Flower Exhibition in London, February 1987.

California, but her colourful style sometimes attracts the wrong sort of publicity. 'No pomp and very little circumstance,' said the *Los Angeles Herald Examiner*; others called them 'the rollicking royals' and criticized the ten-day visit. But Deane Dana, Chairman of the Board of Supervisors of Los Angeles, said their visit had a most positive effect. 'The British people should be proud of their very able and likeable emissaries,' he said – which didn't make a good headline but was far nearer the truth.

'She is rather like a young labrador – untrained as yet but lots of promise,' said one usually reticent courtier, adding, 'one wants to give her an encouraging pat and a cuddle.'

Sometimes she needed just that, especially when the going got rough. At one time there was a great deal of sniping, then, with her pregnancy and the birth of a baby, the pendulum swung her way again. The more experienced royals know this is part of the game and are inclined to be cynical about their fluctuating popularity with the media.

Undoubtedly Fergie can go overboard with her rumbustious personal style. 'She'll have to be careful,' warned a relative of the Queen. But the Duchess seems to have a canny instinct, daily becoming more aware, which keeps her clear of serious mistakes.

When she does overstep the mark Andrew can be tetchy. Like all the family he is a stickler for royal dignity which is, after all, inbred in the Windsor mould. 'You shouldn't have done that,' he said after one boisterous incident with Sarah leading the younger ones into 'unroyal' waters.

Outwardly cheerful and casual she is by nature strong and dominant and usually gets her way. But she does inspire tremendous loyalty from everyone with whom she comes into contact. Her small, overworked staff in the office at Buckingham Palace and at Castlewood House, really do love her and are immensely discreet and protective.

The day aboard USS Nimitz was a highlight of the Yorks' American tour. Sarah, wearing a protective life-jacket and helmet, shares a joke with the captain.

Sarah's personal style on the 1988 US tour earned some criticism, but it didn't mar the welcome the Yorks received in China Town, Los Angeles.

Andrew clearly adores her and she knows how to twist him round her little finger, adorned always with the twin Russian wedding rings he sentimentally gave her before their engagement. They are looking forward to their first real home together when the house the Queen is giving them is built at Sunninghill Park. It is still in construction stage but they hope to move in early in 1990 if all goes according to plan.

The Royal Institute of British Architects has praised the design as 'an unmistakable house of the 1980s,' so perhaps they will try to move in before the end of the decade. It will be the first contemporary royal home since Victoria and Albert built Balmoral as their Scottish retreat. It will be gabled and built of mellowed red brick with a long main wing and two shorter wings forming a courtyard with stables. A high wall will surround the house, screened by poplars and pines, and there will be sophisticated screening devices among other security plans.

The original Sunninghill Park mansion had been destined as a country home for the newly-wed Elizabeth and Philip, now Sarah's in-laws, but it was burned down – to their great disappointment – before they could live in it. So it has given the Queen especial pleasure to present the five-acre site to her son and daughter-in-law as a late wedding present – just as she gave Gatcombe Park to her daughter Anne and Mark Phillips when they were married.

It is estimated that building will cost around £500,000. But the result, on such a valuable site near Windsor Great Park, should be worth at least $1\frac{1}{2}$ million if it is ever sold.

One sentimental touch: at the Queen's suggestion the original wishing well is being kept. She always loved it.

When the Yorks move in everyone is expecting a party to end all parties. Sarah loves entertaining and social events of all kinds. The noise ratio in the magic circle surrounding the Queen increases dramatically when she is around. The younger royals enjoy this because most of them hate the grand, formal parties they sometimes attend. George St Andrews, the Kents' eldest, dreaded them so much he used to feign illness rather than be forced to join the royal ranks.

But it is when 'Ginge', as the favoured are still permitted to call her, is out with some of her many friends in one of her favourite restaurants that the din really crescendos. One of the Queen's staff who was dining quietly in a King's Road trattoria with his wife could not believe his eyes – or his ears – when a typical 'Fergie-set' party arrived in the restaurant.

For a start, the men in pin-striped jackets with jeans brushed the anxious Italian waiters aside and started rearranging the tables. The fourth lady in the land, in a tight leather skirt and bush jacket, sat at the head of one of the tables and supervised, all the time chirping away noisily and easily out-vocalizing the rest of the party.

It has to be said that the 'Fergie set' tends to be noisy and sometimes brash. They can be show-biz, county or jet-set sports-lovers, but they are mostly boisterous and cheerful like Fergie herself. They live in a world that is very small and comprises Belgravia, the King's Road, Chelsea, parts of Battersea and Clapham, and now one of the better addresses in SW1 – Buck House. They migrate to Verbier, several islands in the Caribbean, the Seychelles and wherever there is ski-ing and polo – which could be almost anywhere.

The Princess of Wales would love to be part of this scenario but is actively discouraged by her husband who hates it. Andrew thinks his wife and her friends have fun but cannot always be there to enjoy it because, for much of the time, he is away carrying out his duties in the Navy. When he is around he either enjoys it all thoroughly or 'does a Michael', suddenly turning on the royal dignity and demanding to go home, as does his cousin Prince Michael of Kent when the party gets noisy or out of hand.

Sarah likes to dine out in restaurants or at the home of friends several times a week – although since the birth of her baby she has not minded spending quiet evenings at home.

She always keeps a supply of light ale in the fridge for Glaswegian-born comedian Billy Connolly who, with Pamela Stephenson, are show-biz members of the Set. Another from the theatrical world that seems to fascinate Sarah, is Joan Collins whose dinner party guests these days can include several members of the Royal Family. They were mostly introduced by the Duchess of York who met the actress through David Frost and his wife Carina.

For Andrew, meeting and marrying Sarah has meant a whole new world opening up, as it certainly has for her because, on the face of it, the material gifts to the marriage were all on his side.

How many brides exchange a floral head-dress for a royal tiara when the register has been signed? Or walk up the aisle on the arm of a Major and down on the arm of a Prince of the Realm? Not many young marrieds can look forward to a first home like Sarah's spanking new ranch-style mansion, or a baby whose arrival was heralded by a twenty-one gun salute from Hyde Park and the Tower of London.

Before his wedding, Andrew was lonely despite all the trappings of royalty that had been his since birth. Once at a country house party he said, 'I don't know anyone here . . . I don't really know anyone anywhere.'

Sarah has changed all that. 'She is a real woman,' said Andrew of his Duchess, or as a Canadian put it when she visited his country: 'She sure is a whole lotta woman.'

Left: *A Navy wife in Britain's most famous warship: the Duchess of York in pale-violet, shot-silk evening gown aboard HMS Victory in Portsmouth for an official dinner. Above: The Duke and Duchess of York laugh a lot together. For Andrew, meeting and marrying Sarah has meant a whole new life opening up. She has brought to the marriage an open door to a world few royal princes walk in easily.*

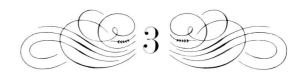

A Twenty-Five-Hour Day

The telephone rang in a small, busy office in the House of Commons. Someone called Sarah Ferguson was on the line to speak to Anna Butcher, the auburn-haired attractive secretary of the then deputy Chief Whip and Royal Treasurer John Stradling-Thomas.

The name raised not a flicker of interest in a room that is renowned as a hive of the latest gossip – be it political, social or royal. To Anna it was a call from an old friend at Queen's Secretarial College in Kensington who wanted her guidance in looking round Westminster. For no one knows 'The People's Palace' better than those who work in it.

But the telephone call was significant because it marked the beginning of a publishing project which, organized by Sarah, would end in a blaze of publicity. Because it was as Duchess of York that, three and a half years later, she launched the glossy *Palace of Westminster* book which she had started working on before her marriage.

It had originally begun with an idea by her boss Richard Burton who hired the ebullient young woman he met at a ski-resort as the London commissioning editor for his Swiss-based publishing firm. He asked her to do some research at the Houses of Parliament and find an author who could tackle the subject. Sarah immediately thought of her friend Anna who had started working for the Welsh MP soon after she left college.

The two red-heads chatted and worked out some guide-lines on how to proceed. Sarah took time to get acquainted with both Houses; she was introduced to the high spot of social life, 'Annie's Bar', and generally absorbed the atmosphere of the Mother of Parliaments.

Through Anna the publisher's editor was introduced to the late Sir Robert Cooke, MP, who had been thinking for some time about writing the history of the two Houses.

Eventually Sarah put together 'a package' which consisted of picking an author (Sir Robert), photographers and designers. The result was a stunning book of which she was extremely proud. 'So she should be,' said Burton at the time. 'It is her baby – the organization was all down to her.'

'I just do the running around, the liaison, the commissioning and making sure everything happens at the right time, at the right place,' was how she explained her job to John Dunne in a BBC radio interview.

Actually Sarah did a formidable amount of work for the author, according to Burton; checking obscure facts and searching out and seeking permission to reproduce pictures.

Burton had originally suggested a book on the palaces and castles of Britain, which Sarah was not keen to handle as it might involve her friendship with the Princess of Wales. She and Diana had become good friends as a result of their constant meetings at Queen's Lawn, Windsor, to watch polo.

It would be unwise, thought Sarah at the time, to jeopardize that friendship. She felt, most strongly, that it would be wrong to use the royal connection in any way to help her job. So Sarah hit on the idea of a book about the only palace which would not involve the Princess; a palace, moreover, in which everyone has an interest.

She still feels that it is important to keep her two lives separate, although they have a habit of dove-tailing into each other in the course of what she jokingly calls 'my twenty-five-hour day.'

Once, going round Dulwich Picture Gallery with Princess Margaret, she spotted an efficient word-processor operator and ended up hiring her for Burton's Swiss office.

Many of her 'Sloane' friends would have found her new role as senior royal Duchess, and position as the fourth lady in the land after the Queen, The Queen Mother and the Princess of Wales, a full-time job. But Sarah has a theory that her own career helps in her work as a senior member of the Royal Family.

As she told one friend: 'it is a good balance – working as hard as I can for both my job and the royal duties. Sometimes, yes, I do burn the candle at both ends. But I'm sure it is good for you – keeps you young.'

Sarah York has steadied down considerably since the days when she was a carefree London working girl, seen here in January 1986.

Three years later she was to be a royal Duchess. Sarah and the Princess of Wales, watching polo at Smith's Lawn, Windsor, in the summer of 1983.

In the office shared by the Yorks and Prince Edward at Buckingham Palace, the girls call her 'a workaholic'. They tell the story of how quiet it all was the first time the Duchess went out of the country with her husband on their highly successful Canadian tour.

Normally Sarah will 'phone home' (as Prince Edward put on their going-away honeymoon landau, from the film E.T.), wherever she is. From doctor, dentist or restaurant Sarah uses her portable phone to speak to the office. 'We miss all the excitement when the Duchess is away,' said one of the staff.

Sarah has always been a livewire, anxious to cram something worthwhile into every moment of the day. All her bosses remember her energy with feeling because she was so hard to replace when she left. One of them, however, remembers something else. 'She spent an awful lot of time on the phone, fixing up her social life,' he said.

Sarah gets up at 6.30 most mornings – even earlier if her baby wakes first. But not before, if possible, 'That would be carrying things too far,' she says. But it is the only way to catch up on her schedules. At the week-ends she sleeps late, if her nanny is around, and if there is no action-woman jaunt afoot like flying, shooting, stalking, or four-in-hand carriage driving – just some of her many interests.

Friends say she has always been constantly on the go; during schooldays at Hurst Lodge, Sunningdale, where she became Head Girl; then at secretarial college where she did a course of shorthand, typing and book-keeping.

Her first job came as a secretary in a flat-letting agency but she soon moved on to become assistant to William Drummond, an art dealer, which stimulated her interest in paintings and the history of art.

Next she had a taste of the PR world which has since proved useful in handling the media in all sorts of situations. Durden-Smith Communications, owned by Neil Durden-Smith, husband of Judith Chalmers the television presenter, found her a useful member of staff who could cope with almost everything that arose – and still smile.

But like most young girls she was restless, always looking for something that interested her more than the present job. At this time she shared a house in Lavender Gardens, near Clapham Junction, with Carolyn Beckwith-Smith (now Mrs Harry Cotterell and mother of a baby daughter, Poppy).

It was there, some time later, that Prince Andrew's Jaguar, with a man inside it, was frequently parked, causing the other residents to fear that their street – fast becoming fashionable – was being 'cased' for a burglary. In fact it was the Queen's second son courting the flame-haired working girl who dashed into her car each morning, briefcase in hand, and came home with carrier bags of goodies to concoct supper for her royal boyfriend. The patient man inside the car was the Prince's long-suffering detective.

'Sarah cooks rather well,' said one of her friends who was a frequent dinner-party guest. 'She learnt originally at some school, but the time she spent on the continent gave her a taste for exquisite food which we've all enjoyed.'

Sarah met Richard Burton, who was to be her next boss, when she was staying in her then-lover Paddy McNally's chalet in Verbier for a ski-ing holiday. Burton obviously felt she had considerable potential and lost no time in assessing the value of this go-ahead, lively young woman and persuading her to join his firm, BCK Graphic Arts, which he'd set up in Switzerland in 1980. He found the quality of Swiss print so good he was soon printing fine art catalogues for Sotheby's and from there he began publishing scholarly books of high quality, mainly for the American market.

That was when Sarah Ferguson came on the scene. After the first meeting with Burton when they were both ski-ing, they met in a more business-like setting in his Geneva office. Except that it rapidly became more informal with Sarah on the floor surrounded by his

Right: *Career girl becomes royal Duchess. Fergie wears a diamond tiara, and diamond and ruby necklace at a dinner in the Duke of York Hotel, Toronto, Canada, in 1987.*

When 'Fergie' was invited to join the Prince and Princess of Wales on a ski-ing holiday to Klosters, it fuelled rumours of an imminent royal engagement.

Right: *Sarah and her close friend Carolyn Beckwith-Smith (now Cotterell), Godmother to Princess Beatrice. She helped 'Fergie' avoid the world's press when rumours of a royal engagement were current.*

pack of four Jack Russell terriers – a breed with which she is entirely familiar. 'Bella' is a family pet at Dummer Down Farm House, her old home; the Waleses have one and Sarah has her own terrier, 'Bendicks', a farewell present from Andrew when he sailed away for their long separation when she was pregnant. The Yorks also have another family pet, 'Tarn', a golden labrador from the Queen's Kennels at Sandringham.

Sarah was excited about her new job and flew back to London to set up an office in Mayfair. Later she was to be besieged there when reporters and photographers from all over the world became alert to her friendship with the Prince.

Earlier, in June 1985, she rang Burton in Geneva to say that she planned to take a few days off for Ascot. What Sarah didn't mention was that she was staying at Windsor Castle in the Queen's house-party as the guest of the Princess of Wales. There she met Andrew again.

Their first meeting, when both were aged ten, had ended in a battle royal because the Queen's son had teased the red-headed tomboy about her red hair. At their first grown-up meeting there was some fooling around over what the couple now call 'those fateful profiteroles'. Sarah, as usual, was on a diet and tried to avert her eyes from all the calorific luxuries brought from the Windsor kitchens to the Royal Box. Andrew, in one of his 'ghastly teasing moods', as the Queen calls them, insisted Sarah tried one of the chocolate confections, oozing with cream from the royal dairies.

'I'm on a diet,' shouted Sarah in a voice rather louder than is usual in the Royal Box. She playfully attempted some fisticuffs with the Prince, which seemed to amuse the Queen.

'She appeared quite glad that someone was standing up to the Prince,' a friend remarked afterwards.

The Royal Family were happy to see Andrew interested in someone else. He had recently broken up with actress Koo Stark after a traumatic last meeting but Sarah was still deeply involved with Paddy McNally, a widower who was years older than herself and had two school-age sons.

She enjoyed meeting Andrew at Ascot but Paddy was still the man in her life when she flew off to meet him for a holiday in Majorca, soon afterwards. But it turned out to be the last time they were together.

Sarah was the marrying kind and friends say she issued an ultimatum to McNally who was still reluctant to wed for a second time. After an emotional scene, according to another guest, they parted and Sarah went home sadly to Clapham to bury herself in work and the hectic social round of a typical 'Sloane' autumn.

Andrew had plenty of leave from his ship HMS *Brazen* which was in British waters. He phoned Sarah for a date and soon became a frequent guest at the dinner parties she and Carolyn shared in Lavender Gardens.

He met some mutual friends on these occasions but was also introduced to Sarah's working world – people she had met through her job, such as writers, photographers, and researchers. None was of the 'rat-pack' species, who would have dearly loved to hear of the budding romance.

That it was becoming serious was obvious to Carolyn. Soon the dinner parties for friends became suppers *à deux*, and Carolyn, madly in love with the man who was to become her husband, Harry Cotterell, was sympathetic to the hints that Sarah would like to be alone with Andrew.

About this time had come the disquieting news that the author she had chosen to write the Westminster book, then well under way, was becoming seriously ill with motor neurone disease which was to prove fatal. He was coping with work on the book by dictating into a machine but Sarah was desperately worried about him. She was torn between wanting to see the work brought to a satisfactory conclusion and sorrow that Sir Robert should be spending the last months of his life working so hard.

'I kept willing him to stop because I could not bear the thought of poor Lady Cooke and Sir Robert in their last months having to worry about it,' she said later. But he was determined to finish it and with the help of Dr Penelope Hunting, his researcher, he almost did complete the work.

Sarah helped all she could. When she was on honeymoon at Balmoral she was still working and even sent Sir Robert some material she had collated, which he thought remarkably efficient.

Andrew was not so surprised. Before their wedding plans were finally settled and that ruby engagement ring was on her finger, Sarah had made it clear her work was important to her and she wanted to continue to have a career of her own. The Queen found it a novel idea but agreed – even to the extent of allowing Sarah to set up her office at Buckingham Palace because the Royal Protection Squad were in a panic about security in her office in Central London.

Clearly, however, it was a situation that could not continue. A commercial enterprise carried on under the Queen's roof could only be a very temporary measure.

It helped Sarah over a difficult situation, at the time, as she was still extremely busy with the Westminster project, especially when the tragic death of Sir Robert meant that all hands were needed to steer it through to the publication deadline.

After the book's launch when Sarah helped promote it by appearing on television and radio, she resigned from Burton's company – it is believed on Palace advice.

It was just as well, perhaps, as the Swiss firm was dissolved in 1988 with what were reported to be financial problems. It was just the sort of bogey that the Queen and the Duke of Edinburgh had felt could be one of the hazards of their young branching out in different commercial directions. But, as Sarah was no longer employed by Burton, there was no way in which she was involved. Palace advisers breathed easily but it was reckoned a close one.

'The Duchess will freelance in future,' said a spokesman firmly, 'from her own home at Castlewood House.'

Sarah and Andrew moved into the seven-roomed house conveniently close to Windsor Castle and the Guards' Polo Club where Major Ronald Ferguson was then to be found most days, just before Christmas 1988.

The house, loaned by the Royal Family's good friend King Hussein of Jordan, is a veritable fortress where Sarah will be able to work undisturbed on new projects, until their new, modern home is built at Sunninghill Park.

King Hussein originally took over Castlewood more than ten years ago and used it occasionally as a base for his children and their staff. When in Britain, Hussein and his lovely wife Queen Noor live at nearby Buckhurst Park, which adjoins Windsor Great Park. The two royal families see each other frequently and Queen Noor is a keen spectator at Smith's Lawn polo ground where she is often to be seen chatting to the Princess of Wales while their children play together.

Sarah's temporary home, where she spent the long, lonely last months of her pregnancy when Andrew was away on his ship heading towards the Southern Hemisphere, had been already well protected by the security-conscious King Hussein. But when the Yorks moved in, a further hefty sum was spent on it, on the advice of the Royal Protection Squad.

Castlewood now has direct telephone links with all local police stations and Scotland Yard, survey cameras everywhere and armed guards at all times. 'I never had this in Lavender Gardens,' laughed Sarah to Diana as the two of them tried to ensure that William

Opposite: *The day of her engagement; at a Buckingham Palace photo-call 'Fergie' shows off her ruby and diamond ring designed by Andrew.*

Above: *The King and Queen of Jordan have loaned the Yorks a house on the fringes of Windsor Great Park until their own is ready. Here Queen Noor, a keen spectator at polo, watches with the Duke of York.*

and Harry of Wales did not barge into any sensitive equipment.

She has an office, complete with typewriter and dictating equipment, on the ground floor of the house overloooking the gardens, where she holds meetings sometimes. But if several people are involved Sarah will meet them in London, usually in a hotel or restaurant. On one occasion she met two colleagues at the busy Carlton Tower Hotel in London, unnoticed by tourists from all over the world. 'If people don't expect to see me, they don't usually notice I'm there,' she explained on one occasion to a researcher who expressed surprise that the Duchess of York was attracting so little attention.

David Frost asked her, after the publication of *Palace of Westminster*, in a TV-am interview, how she coped with her two roles. 'The real thing about it is I can do it because I think the busier you are the more you get done.

'For me it is a tonic. It keeps me in touch with the world round me. It takes about twenty-five hours a day – but I just make sure there is time.

'The girls in the office insist I'm a workaholic. It drives them mad but I just do it and want to do it.

'At the end of the day when Andrew comes home I have done something too. I haven't been sitting there wondering what I am going to put on the next day.'

Sarah has considered doing a book about George III's collection of 2,000 Italian architectural drawings in the Royal Library at Windsor. The King was a great collector and a fine artist who particularly liked the precision of architectural drawings. The Italian collection was among the first treasures the Queen showed her new daughter-in-law and they were both very keen for her to embark on the project. Sarah did begin sorting out the drawings with the advice of the Professor of the History of Architecture at Harvard University, Howard Burns. But the project was shelved during her pregnancy and is in 'the pending file'.

'Fergie' counts zany actress Pamela Stephenson, wife of Glaswegian comedian Billy Connolly as one of her closest friends. The couple are part of the 'show-biz' element in the 'Fergie-set'.

Another idea she has is a book about the historic exhibits in the Israel Museum in Jerusalem. But, as it involved travel to the Middle East, it too was postponed.

Naturally, like anyone else in her profession, she is not anxious to discuss impending work as she is in a very competitive business. A book has to be well on the way before she'll talk about it and even then she is reluctant to give away too many details.

Sarah works hard, but she always finds time for the light-hearted moments. Her first job for Burton was a text book on the Impressionists – a fine art book called *The New Painting*. To get the package together Sarah researched all experts in the field and came up with the senior curator of San Francisco Museum who was, according to Sarah herself, quite difficult to sign up.

She flew to America, contacted the historian and invited him out to lunch. Over a fiery curry, which they thoroughly enjoyed, a deal was struck. It resulted in a book which eventually sold 155,000 copies in Britain and the United States.

Sarah freely admits she could not go on working without the support and understanding of her husband. On the back of the Westminster book was a photograph he took of her which has become a favourite of them both. As she put it to her friend David Frost, the picture was taken by 'a very exciting young photographer.' He was, she said 'absolutely incredible ... exceptionally good-looking and really, actually my support, my main right arm ... my husband of course.'

Opposite: The York family. Beatrice was christened in December 1988.

4

Being Royal is No Big Deal

The ghosts of the unhappy women once locked up in his home do not appear to worry the Queen's nephew David Linley as he potters happily around his 'pad' in Fulham, once a women's prison. The three main rooms bear no hints of bars, chains or bowls of prisoners' gruel. Instead the strains of Lloyd Cole and the Commotions or the Rolling Stones and other favourites swing out from his collection of compact discs. And a delicious fragrance of the exotic food David loves steals out of his kitchen/dining room where he cooks whilst talking to dinner guests.

Viscount Linley, twenty-seven, son of Princess Margaret and Lord Snowdon, is enjoying his life on the other side of the palace walls where he grew up. Like his sister and cousins he has some of the privileges of his ancestry without having to pay the price of royal birthright in terms of personal freedom. For although Princess Margaret insists her children are not royal – 'they just happen to have the Queen as an aunt' – doors have a way of opening for these grandchildren of King George VI and Queen Elizabeth the Queen Mother. David Linley concedes this but points out, 'Being royal is no big deal here in London.'

He is a solemn young man whose wide smiles are as rare as the crumbs of royal information he occasionally drops, 'My mother is very artistic,' or, 'my sister and I ...' Growing up in such a family circle he learnt early the art of brusque discretion and wears the royal mantle of personal privacy to the manner born. But he is by no means as uncomplicated as he would appear. It is true he started off as a genuine royal 'chippy', but now he is deeply into the commercial business of making money.

His apparent aestheticism is balanced by a high-achieving urge for success; his personal style flip-flops from grave, sedate demi-royal to breezy Bohemian man-about-town – laced usually with charm but occasionally with the casual arrogance of a royal fledgling.

David Albert Charles entered the world on 3 November 1961, at his grandmother's home, Clarence House, under the astrological sign of Scorpio, like his first cousin the Prince of Wales with whom he is close. Other royal Scorpios are the Princess Royal's son, Peter Phillips, and the Earl of Ulster, the Duke and Duchess of Gloucester's son.

'The Princess and I are absolutely thrilled and delighted,' the new baby's father told waiting journalists. The Queen arrived with armfuls of flowers for her sister and the family toasted the new arrival with champagne beneath the Waterford crystal chandeliers in the Queen Mother's elegant Nash-designed drawing room.

David Linley makes hand-crafted furniture of exceptional quality. He says, 'I don't think one ought to be doing this kind of work if money were the most important thing.'

David's childhood in another royal home, Kensington Palace, was to be an entirely normal one for a princess's son, with the disciplined routine of Nanny Sumner's nursery regime and early lessons with his cousins in the schoolroom at Buckingham Palace. But in his young adulthood he was notable for breaking the established mould for royal offspring by setting himself up as an artisan.

Now he manages to glean the best of both worlds: riding in a royal landau in grey topper and morning suit in the Queen's procession to Ascot or astride his bicycle on the way to work through Chelsea streets with stereophonic sound plugged into both ears. David loves music – anything from pop to his mother's favourite ballet. Like her he plays the piano well and is noted for a lively interpretation of Scott Joplin.

He is a devotee of anything mechanical that is fast – motorcars or bikes – as his brushes with the law for speeding offences testify. He is also a great lover of gadgets, particularly for his kitchen. When he accompanied his mother and sister to China they stopped off in Hong Kong and David took them gadget-hunting.

Davy Jones, as he is known down the King's Road, Chelsea, is making a lucrative success of both his careers: carpenter/furniture-maker and restaurateur. And he is loving every moment of freedom from the royal destiny that has trapped his mother since birth. Indeed, business is flourishing to such an extent that David could be well on his way to becoming the first royal millionaire actually to earn – and not inherit – the banknotes with his aunt's head on them.

A future in the commercial world was far away when he was christened in the Music Room of Buckingham Palace. Like all the royal babies he wore the robe of cream satin and Honiton lace in which Queen Victoria's children were christened, and every royal child since.

Nanny Sumner, who was very much of the old school, ruled the nursery domain and, with young first cousins in Buckingham Palace, it was natural that David spent a lot of time there. It became almost a second home, with either the country residences of the Queen or the Queen Mother as the background to most weekends and holidays.

He joined the Palace schoolroom at five years old for lessons with Miss Katherine Peebles ('Mispy') who had taught Prince Charles and Princess Anne. Before that she had been governess to Princess Alexandra and Prince Michael of Kent, but now she had charge of Prince Andrew and his younger cousin David.

Later on they both went to Gibbs, the London school, and David graduated to Ashdown Preparatory School, which was conveniently near a cottage on the Nymans estate of his paternal ancestors. Lord Snowdon had recently renovated it as a weekend home and David used to spend his 'leave-outs' from school there or at one of the royal homes.

David turned out to be hopeless at lessons. 'A determined duffer,' one of his teachers described him. Princess Margaret told her sister how worried she was about his work and the Queen went down to Sussex to see her nephew and try and encourage him. As a result he did much better and won a prize for general knowledge, largely because he knew the name of the Prime Minister and the architect of St Paul's – both drilled into him in the schoolroom at Buckingham Palace.

He had piano lessons at Ashdown and has enjoyed playing ever since, particularly jazz. But even in those days he was a keen carpenter and made the Queen and Princess Margaret bird boxes for Christmas.

When the Snowdon children were growing up in the shadow of their parents' divorce, the Queen took them under her wing and they became part of her own young family.

It was becoming all too clear that he would never pass the entrance exams to Eton, his father's old school. Instead he was sent to Millbrook House, a pre-public school 'crammer'. This prepared him for Bedales, the progressive co-educational school in Hampshire which he entered when he was thirteen. David's eleven-year-old sister Sarah joined him at the school, which turned out to be a successful move for both of them as they were very happy there.

It was just as well Bedales provided a stable background because their home life was not easy at this time. Both parents were nervy and edgy with each other and it soon became obvious that their marriage was running into grave trouble. As is always the case, it was a particularly upsetting time for their children, as Christopher Warwick described in his official biography *Princess Margaret* when he wrote about the last holiday they all shared in Italy.

'It was a disaster for no sooner had they arrived than Tony fell into one of his silences. "Papa, Mummy is talking to you," one of the children would say. "I know," was all he replied.

'Then at the end of the first week, as the Princess recalls, Snowdon packed his bag and returned to London leaving her with David and Sarah to continue their holiday alone.'

The Queen was a great comfort at this time. She took the Snowdon children under her wing and they became part of her own young family, sharing holidays in the royal homes or on the yacht.

The school authorities were aware of the situation and efforts were made to stimulate the children's interest in creative recreation so that they were always absorbed and busy.

Princess Margaret and Lord Snowdon certainly appear to have chosen the right school for their children. Edward Barnsley, one of the best of modern furniture designers, was an old boy and the school has always encouraged the creative arts. At home both his mother and his aunt tried to foster David's love of furniture. The Queen showed him her priceless Georgian pieces and introduced him to her craftsmen at Marlborough House who are constantly repairing and restoring royal furniture. The workshops became a favourite place for David in the holidays, followed by tea with his grandmother at Clarence House or his aunt and cousins at Buckingham Palace.

At Bedales, David, who had first developed an interest in making things in his father's workshop at Kensington Palace, used to disappear into the school workshops to work on the lathes. This creativity, which he says comes from both sides of his family, was encouraged at the school who also educated the gifted Matthew Rice, now David's partner and close friend in the furniture making business.

So absorbed was David in the study of wood that he decided to try for Parnham House, the woodcraft school run by the great British wood-carver John Makepeace. There was stiff competition for a place as apprentice but he eventually signed on for a two-year course.

Furniture-makers have always felt they were the poor relations of architects and sculptors, but John Makepeace's school for Craftsmen in Wood emphasizes that apprentices are learning a craft which is a living heritage every bit as enduring as other art forms. His school has produced several of Britain's leading young designers in wood who, like David, find themselves in a thriving market. Most of the work is commissioned and it is an expensive but very worthwhile project for the clients.

At the end of the two years, students exhibited their best pieces. David, ever practical, as the royals find at Christmas, showed a wooden loo-roll holder as one of his prize efforts, much to the amusement of his mother who came to admire.

David Linley, Furniture-maker, set up business in a converted bakery at Dorking, Surrey, with two friends working as a co-operative. He began work only two days after leaving Parnham House because, already ambitious, he wanted to waste no time in making some money.

'I had a two-day break after finishing school because it was the weekend. We had the rent to pay. We had to start making money as soon as possible … I was entirely self-financed,' he said of those early days in his career.

By now his parents had resolved their difficulties and, though divorced, were friendly in a civilized fashion that made life so much easier for their children. They both enthusiastically encouraged David as he began serious wood-making projects working on a 'rainbow' table and 'rainbow' screens – a design that was to become his trade-mark.

Princess Margaret found herself looking for conspicuous places among her lovely possessions to show off examples of David's work. Her own antique dining table was moved out to accommodate one hand-crafted by her son upon which the Princess wined and dined until he requested it back to give to Charles and Diana as a wedding present.

The first major break came when a London exhibition gave him the opportunity to try something really special. He called it an 'olé chest' and shaped it like a Shinto shrine in sycamore, the milky-white wood which polishes up to a lustre like ivory. It is a wood he really loves and he designed the doors of the chest imaginatively with different coloured leather.

David was naturally desperately anxious for his first *magnum opus* to be a success. A royal child – and even a semi-royal one – has to try twice as hard as anyone else, as Princess Anne found with competitive show-jumping. And when a youngster bred from Windsor stock is also a great-nephew of multi-talented Oliver Messel, the theatrical designer, and comes from a long line of artistic Linleys, including Linley Sambourne, one of the greatest black-and-white artists at the turn of the century, it is doubly important to succeed.

David, at that time, was probably not conscious of his illustrious ancestors, although he certainly is now. Always understated, he only says, 'My parents are both very artistic, but I think any talents I have come from my father's side.'

He worked day and night over that olé chest, often helped by his friend and colleague Charles Wheeler-Carmichael, one of the partners in the co-operative. Then, cradling it in his arms, he sat in the back of a rented van while Charles drove them to London. With every bump in the road David held the chest closer until they reached the site of the exhibition. There he and Charles carried it up two flights of stairs and finally, rather optimistically, placed a price tag of £2,500 on the polished wood.

Princess Margaret dropped in to see 'the masterpiece' and was clearly delighted and secretly impressed. So was the client who paid the price and took home what will almost certainly be an antique in the future. David came away from the exhibition with several orders and does not seem to have looked back since. Sensibly he invested his earnings in some expensive tools which he had not been able to afford before.

Soon he moved to a new workshop at Betchworth and the family came down for opening day, including Princess Margaret, Lady Sarah Armstrong-Jones, Lord Snowdon and his second wife, Lucy. Everyone clapped as the Princess, with David's help, used a large saw to cut a silver ribbon and wished the new workshop great good fortune.

As new horizons began to open up, David teamed up with his old schoolfriend Matthew Rice who was, by now, an extremely talented artist. They opened their doors at No. 1, New King's Road, Chelsea, in 1985, and several members of the Royal Family, including Princess Margaret, Lady Sarah Armstrong-Jones, the Duchess of Kent, Lady Helen Windsor and the Ogilvys attended the launching party.

The team of Linley and Rice is unique in that it combines David's excellent wood-working with Matthew's delicate water-colour designs and feeling for colour. Each time a

Below: *David loves clothes and like his mother, Princess Margaret, enjoys dressing up. He helped organize the RAJ ball for charity with his sister, girlfriend Susannah Constantine and a friend.*

Above: *Linley is enthusiastic about anything mechanical that is fast. Here, in a rare public engagement when he was younger, he opened a new MGB owner's club.*

Left: *Funtime. David likes dancing and pop concerts or going to the ballet. He danced the night away in the Hippodrome ballroom at the RAJ ball wearing an exotic outfit with snazzy mandarin jacket complete with diamond brooch.*

client commissions a piece of furniture Matthew does an exquisite water-colour of the design for him to study. They have customers in Japan, Australia, Canada, Europe and the USA.

Their use of fine marquetry is a feature of the designs, such as the huge bed, twelve feet square, which they made for the singer Elton John and his wife Renate in happier days before their marriage break up. After it was delivered, the Queen and Princess Margaret drove over to Crimp Hill, Old Windsor, to see it.

'The Queen was absolutely thrilled with David's work,' said a relative. 'She takes a great interest in both her sister's children because they are so close to her.' Princess Margaret made her son smile when she remarked on the bed, 'I wish you'd stop calling it a piece of furniture. It's a room!'

The family have watched David's work progress from the wooden boxes he used to make as Christmas presents to the more intricate and beautiful workmanship of today. By 1987 – two years after the partnership began – David and Matthew had their first custom-crafted furniture exhibited in the US.

Undeniably his royal background helped to get the business off the ground. 'Certainly it opens doors and one does know people,' agrees David. 'But those doors will slam in your face if you don't deliver the goods.'

When interviewed he speaks very cautiously, weighing every word. At times he is monosyllabic and often closes up completely. He only really warms up with strangers when his furniture is praised. 'Do you like it? Do you really?' he asks, and the apparent arrogance that was present a moment ago when asked a question about his family is gone and there is an appealing diffidence and even trace of humility.

Princess Margaret's son is a mixture of different personalities. 'He has all his mother's strength,' said a relative. 'He is shy, which is unlike her, but his flashpoint is low, which is similar.'

David's eyes can flash just like Princess Margaret's when he thinks someone has gone too far. The Windsor chin juts out and the conversation comes to an abrupt halt. As someone, who had just experienced it, said, 'There is a decided feeling that one ought to exit from the scene – backwards.' Except that it is only Davy Jones, and the put-down doesn't quite carry the same weight as when it comes from his aunt or mother.

His friends agree it is not easy to get close to David. Those who do are aware that he can be a chameleon character. Dining once with actress Joan Collins he started out shy and taciturn, but by the end of dinner he had blossomed under his hostess's very considerable charms and was the life and soul of the party. But he can easily become morose and withdrawn. Like his father, Lord Snowdon, he can also be extremely vague. 'But that is really a red herring,' said one friend. 'He is really quite cleverly avoiding an issue he doesn't want to talk about. Like all the young royals he is shy and longs to be private, but when he trusts someone there is nobody more loving and generous.'

David has had a roving eye in his time but his most permanent amour, certainly at one time, was his on/off girlfriend, the beautiful Susannah Constantine, who is a great favourite of his mother and grandmother. Princess Margaret has invited her to Mustique and the Queen Mother likes David to bring her to Royal Lodge for the weekend.

Susannah is in fashion PR – and is very successful. David, a dedicated careerist, admires her professionalism. She is very much in the young royal set. Helen Windsor was at school with her at St Mary's, Wantage, and David's sister is a great friend.

Susannah shares a Battersea flat with her old schoolfriend Lulu Blacker who is very close to the Duchess of York. When others in the set are asked to address her as 'Ma'am' Lulu still calls her by the personal nickname she has always used. Sarah York is 'Ginge' and Lulu is called 'Blackbush' by the Duchess.

David's royal world: escorting the Queen Mother, Princess Margaret and the Princess Royal through the royal enclosure at Ascot in 1988.

Susannah and David met in 1983 when she was on a teaching course in London, and he gave her an engagement ring on St Valentine's Day 1987. But, friends say, a furious lovers' quarrel ended the unofficial engagement.

For someone who has been brought up in a palace, David is extraordinarily happy in his own small Fulham home. It stirs something, perhaps, from another part of his ancestry for it is not far from the terraced house in Kensington where his great-great-grandfather Edward Linley Sambourne – from whose name David takes his title – lived with his wife Marion.

Linley Sambourne was a leading *Punch* cartoonist at the beginning of the century. His house in Stafford Terrace, an evocative example of the Victorian style, is now owned by the Royal Borough of Kensington and Chelsea and is open to the public. It was recently photographed by Lord Snowdon.

David's great-great-grandmother Marion would not have had the twentieth-century gadgets in her kitchen that he has, but in her comparatively modest house she had four servants. David has a daily who comes in to clean for him and make his bed if he has forgotten. But usually he looks after himself very well. For breakfast he likes boiled eggs, and drinks either coffee or the green China tea he was introduced to when he and his sister accompanied Princess Margaret on her tour of China and the Far East.

Linley and Marion Sambourne made their home a reflection of their personalities with door panels painted by the artist and his own drawings on the walls. Their great-great-grandson has also reflected himself in his own way. 'Your home should be a representation of your style,' he believes. For David that means a strong hint of his liking for privacy, with warm dark claret walls in the drawing room, which make a rich background for his collection of contemporary paintings, some of which are by his partner Matthew; others by the American artist Wege Deliss.

David has planned this setting for his home life to have a 'country feel', especially in the kitchen/dining room for which he has made a cleverly designed glass-topped table so that eight guests can sit round it. He felt an all-wood table would be overpowering in the small space available, but reckons this one will spend its time being moved around to display to customers or at exhibitions. Princess Margaret lends him a table – usually an antique with Georgian painted chairs – when his own is away, and, with all the furniture moving, David and Matthew have become expert removal men.

When they were in China Sarah encouraged her brother's interest in water-colour painting, which he finds relaxing. One of the memories of the tour was the day they took their paints and brushes and settled down, complete with 'minders', in the middle of a paddy field.

But usually it is his cameras that accompany him everywhere. Lord Snowdon was responsible for the great interest all the young royals have in photography. Like his ancestor Linley Sambourne, who used to photograph subjects before turning them into a cartoon, David uses his as a useful adjunct to work. If he is visiting a client's home, he takes along one of the cameras in case he forgets what the room looks like when he is making the furniture.

Queen Mary always used to advise her grandchildren, Elizabeth and Margaret, to have inquiring minds. She believed that to be inquisitive reaped its own reward in the knowledge thus acquired. The Princess passed this advice on to her children and they are both exceptionally alert and aware – a valuable asset in careers that are so dependent on fine detail.

For one who is frequently so casually dressed, David enjoys clothes and has strong views on what he likes. He has been through his 'punk' period when he turned up on a royal occasion with bleached hair and an overcoat three sizes too large. Now he is quietly conservative for formal occasions in suits by Douglas Hayward or off-the-peg from Paul Smith. He loves going off to Covent Garden with his sister, wandering round the many small shops there.

Like the Princess of Wales he likes to fit in a swim every day but he doesn't join her in the Palace pool. Instead he'll slip into a local Chelsea swimming baths where he eases out the day's tensions with a strong breast stroke.

Later on it is playtime – he likes dancing and pop concerts or going to the ballet. Or his late evenings might be spent cooking for friends or dining out with them, sometimes in 'Deals', the restaurant he owns jointly with his cousin Lord Lichfield in the new Chelsea Marina complex. As it is so near his shop, David calls it his 'works caff'. It reminds one of those small, bustling restaurants to be found on Rhode Island where the Transatlantic yachts finish, or anywhere on the New England coast. But this restaurant is a short walk from King's Road, Chelsea, and has a clientele ranging from the fashionable glitterati to tie-less workmen doing overtime on the building site all around it. It is reasonably cheap – between £10–£15 a head – and features the sort of food David himself enjoys: beefburgers, spring rolls, satay fondu, steaks and plenty of tomato ketchup which he adores.

As Princess Margaret's son he has, of course, been brought up on exquisite food and is genuinely interested in it. He loves cooking like he enjoys making furniture and his speciality is salmon mousse (without tomato ketchup). In all likelihood the fish is caught in the royal waters of the Dee.

He and Lord Lichfield have been eating together for years. They collect food books, and sometimes wander from cafe to restaurant on holiday, often in France. They clearly get on well and have hit on the idea of serving the kind of food that is somewhere between a cafeteria and a more expensive trattoria.

The name 'Deals' comes from David, Eddy and Lichfield. Eddy Lim is chef and *restaura-*

teur, and co-owner with Lichfield of another London restaurant 'Tai Pan'. Lords Lichfield and Linley hope 'Deals' is the start of a restaurant chain. They already have plans for another on London's river and hope eventually to span Britain, giving the country a taste of the exotic. It's all a long way from the spotless white tablecloth and bland food in Nanny Sumner's nursery at Kensington Palace where David longed for spicy sauces to liven things up.

As with the restaurant, anyone can visit the small shop in Chelsea to inspect his wares. They are not all as big as the 55-foot-long table of English oak he made for the boardroom of the Metropolitan Museum in New York. It was a tremendous accolade winning the order as it was unlikely the museum was particularly impressed with Linley's royal connections. They put the job out to tender and David and Matthew won the contract.

David and his partner Matthew Rice, a talented artist, drew inspiration from Venice when they designed their range of china and glass.

Princess Margaret is a great supporter of her son's commercial career. Here she attends a party at jewellers Mappin and Webb to launch a new range of china and glass by David Linley Ltd.

David Linley and Matthew Rice have a five-year plan for their company and are always coming up with new ideas. But they say there are not enough hours in the day to do it all!

The table was made from oaks cut in Windsor Great Park so it has a royal pedigree like its maker. 'We know where each tree came from,' said David. He also made sure the moisture content was correct for the air conditioning in New York and the extremes of climate. It was made in their Gloucestershire workshop and will seat sixty people. David reckons it is certainly one of the largest made this century.

Most of David's projects are costly these days. But some are within an average price range. There are stationery sets, chessboards, letter-racks, jotters and pencil pots based on Matthew's water-colour sketches of Venice. They sell at around £30 each.

At a recent exhibition some of his major work was displayed to contrast with furniture by George Hepplewhite. It delighted David but awed him slightly as well. 'It is very flattering to be compared with him and my work is built to last. I hope it will be handed down from generation to generation,' he said.

It also gave him a terrific 'buzz' when the Victoria and Albert Museum commissioned his contemporary furniture made from hurricane-damaged trees, and Mappin and Webb asked him to make a collection of china and glass.

'Everything is exciting and hectic,' he said; the puckish grin, so like his father's, lighting up his face.

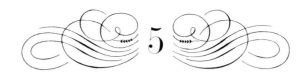

ℐ Passionate Painter

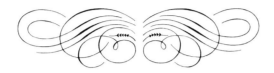

When Princess Margaret was her daughter's age one of her closest friends described her as 'a bird in a gilded cage. She would have loved to break free but was never able to.'

Like her brother, Sarah grew up with Nanny Sumner's words constantly repeated, 'Always remember you are royal children.' But now she has firmly rejected public duties and life 'in the gilded cage' to become an extremely liberated young artist.

Princess Margaret has strongly emphasized her daughter is not one of the royal team. 'She will not undertake public engagements or take on official duties. She is an entirely private person and not a member of the Royal Family.' Yet Sarah is very much an integral and much loved member of the most famous family in the world. The Queen, who helped bring her up, treats her like another daughter; the Princess of Wales looks on her as one of her closest friends, making her not only her chief bridesmaid but also godmother to Prince Harry.

Sarah herself happily exchanges the easy-going life of her artist friends for the protocol-monitored court surrounding her aunt, and has a deep love and commitment to the Queen and her family which will probably restrain the more emancipated aspects of her life-style.

Though she often dresses in the comfortable baggy clothes of a typical art student, with her long hair in a pigtail down her back, and has learnt to lose herself in a crowd, a closer look betrays the royal relationship. She has the same distinctive feathered eyebrows of the Queen and the Queen Mother, the vivid blue eyes of her mother and aunt and an uncanny resemblance to them both – especially in her expressions when talking.

As a teenager, unsettled by her parents' marital problems, she became the Queen's shadow and her aunt was immensely protective of the youngster who clung closely to her side. They still love each other's company and keep closely in touch by telephone when they cannot meet.

The variety of clothes hanging in Sarah's bedroom in the small South Kensington house she moved into from her mother's home at Kensington Palace, significantly emphasizes the different worlds, so far apart, in which she lives. Earlier she had been rather a disappointment to Princess Margaret who has always adored dressing up both for everyday and special occasions. But, blossoming in the happiness of a love affair with good-looking actor Daniel Chatto, Sarah has been wearing some really lovely outfits – much to her mother's pleasure

Left: *Dressed up in a Victor Edelstein ball gown for a formal royal night out, Sarah wears diamonds round her neck and in her ears, and coils her long hair into an elegant style for a party at Claridges for ex-King Constantine of Greece.*

Right: *By day Sarah loves wearing her student gear – jeans, loose sweater and casual jacket – at art school.*

and relief. However, she still loves her student clothes for day-to-day wear when she is painting – or when she turns up at a 'bring a bottle' party in someone's flat or digs.

Anna Harvey, fashion director of *Vogue* magazine who helped Diana find her clothes style, has been guiding Sarah recently. Like the Princess of Wales, who suggested she asked Anna's advice, Sarah popped into the *Vogue* offices and watched them select clothes to photograph. Then Anna helped her pick outfits for formal occasions when Sarah is with the Royal Family or out on the town with Daniel. The result has been stunning, transforming her – much to her surprise – into a perfect complement to her cousin Helen's blonde loveliness. 'Snow White and Rose Red', quipped one of a group of admirers when they stepped out together.

Her brother also takes an interest in her clothes. He loves shopping and he and Sarah go off to Covent Garden with a group of friends and wander round the boutiques. Then they stop at a bistro for coffee, drinks or the green tea David loves and can rarely find in London except in a Chinese restaurant.

Sarah and Helen Windsor, daughter of the Duke and Duchess of Kent, were two of a quartet of royal births in 1964. 'A royal population explosion' or 'palace procreation' as author Robert Lacey put it, and they have been friends since babyhood.

When Sarah Frances Elizabeth Armstrong-Jones was born, three days after Helen, on 1st May, her parents planted a climbing red rose in their garden at Kensington Palace to mark the event.

She arrived by Caesarean section, like the Queen, whose birth sign of Taurus Sarah shares – her friend Helen was also born under this sign. Princess Margaret chose the date as appropriate for her baby, signifying happiness and the coming of spring. It was a well-chosen birthday for a child who is so universally loved. 'She is an absolute sweetheart,' said a relative. 'A really lovely girl,' commented her lodger Dominic Best; 'the most normal, down to earth character you could meet,' said George Hatton, who first taught her to paint.

From the start her parents have encouraged her to be free of the royal yolk just as they did with her brother David. After schoolroom days at Buckingham Palace with Prince Edward and James Ogilvy – the other half of the quartet – she went to London's Frances Holland School for Girls.

As a ten-year-old she attended Monday evening classes at the Royal Ballet School under the tuition of Dame Ninette de Valois and has adored ballet ever since. It is a love she shares with her friend the Princess of Wales and her mother, Princess Margaret, Patron of the London Festival Ballet.

When Sarah was eleven her mother and father – then at the height of their marital friction – decided to send her with David to Bedales School. She was two years younger than most of the children there but settled in very happily.

Sarah attends the wedding of her cousin James Ogilvy to Julia Rawlinson.

During her teens Sarah, unsettled by her parents' marital problems, became the Queen's shadow, and her aunt was immensely protective of the youngster who kept close to her side whenever possible.

The Queen, deeply sensitive to the trauma of the Snowdons' marriage split-up, became a sheet-anchor for Sarah giving her the stable home background she needed in those vulnerable adolescent years. Holidays were spent in the heart of the Royal Family who all did their utmost to cheer her up. She and David grew to know and love Windsor, Sandringham and Balmoral as well as any of them. They sailed and scuba-dived from the royal yacht; learnt to fish alongside their grandmother, the Queen Mother, and Prince Charles, and scrambled miles over rocky terrain with the Queen on deer-stalking expeditions.

Once a year they visited the Castle of Mey, the Queen Mother's remote summer home in Caithness. The royal yacht anchored off-shore and the children came ashore with the Queen and Prince Philip to spend the day at Mey. They particularly loved collecting shells on the beach and listened, fascinated, as their grandmother told them that if they stood very still and sang the old Scottish ballads, the seals might come in to hear them – as they often did for the royal owner of the castle.

When they eventually reached Balmoral, Sarah was never as interested in the daily expeditions as the boys were. Even then she would take her sketch-book along and produce creativity out of a day mainly dedicated to sport by the others in the family. In the evening she'd show her drawings to the Queen in the way Queen Victoria and her daughters used to compare their artistic efforts after a day on the hill or by the river.

Sarah took her sketch-book back to school as part of a holiday exercise. 'We never pried,' said her teacher George Hatton. 'Yet you knew that she had been up sketching at Balmoral or Sandringham during the holidays. But she made nothing of her royal background.' Like all royal youngsters, Sarah learnt early to submerge her 'other life' and never talked about her relatives.

Sarah passed seven O levels and an A level in art. She knew then that, more than anything, she wanted a career in an art-orientated job. George Hatton encouraged her in this, 'She is a natural painter with a great facility to express herself,' he said. 'She should make a good professional artist.'

At Bedales the art class kept one of Sarah's paintings – a still life – to show to future pupils. The Queen has several and particularly likes some of the early ones; sketches of wild flowers – honeysuckle, poppies and dog-roses – drawn in the meadows round Sandringham.

According to former boyfriend Cosmo Fry, 'Painting is her great passion. Her favourite medium is water-colour. She likes to disappear into the countryside with her sketch pad and paint landscapes and flowers.'

Painting is in Sarah's blood on both sides of the family. Queen Victoria was a prolific artist as Jane Roberts, Curator of the Print Room at Windsor Castle, points out in her book *Royal Artists*. 'Literally thousands of drawings survive from her hand, ranging throughout her long life, and each of her children was taught to paint and draw proficiently.' Among Victoria's drawings in the Archives is a copy of one of Raphael's male nudes done in 1860 when she was forty-one. A portrait of a nubian by her eldest daughter, the Princess Royal, later Empress of Prussia, is reminiscent of a charcoal drawing by Sarah which was chosen to hang in the Royal Academy in 1988.

In past centuries the monarch had a drawing master as a member of the Household and royal children were expected to be artistic. They used the skills thus acquired rather as the Queen and her family use photography today – to illustrate and record events at home and abroad on their travels.

Like her brother, Sarah is especially close to her grandmother, the Queen Mother, who is also an art lover. Sarah appreciates greatly her small – by royal standards – but glorious collection kept at Clarence House, Royal Lodge and the Castle of Mey.

Princess Margaret advised her daughter not to say much in public. 'I have suffered from my own early quotes all my life,' the Princess once said.

George III, Queen Charlotte and the royal children all painted. The King was extremely accomplished and left many drawings of architecture and design in which he was especially interested. Queen Victoria's fourth daughter, Louise, later Duchess of Argyll, was the most professional of her generation and the first member of the Royal Family to exhibit her work at the Royal Academy.

Of the next generation Princess Patricia of Connaught (Lady Patricia Ramsay) exhibited frequently in London and Canada, and Queen Mary, Marina Duchess of Kent and the Princess Royal all showed their work in public exhibitions. But they were amateur artists. Sarah aims to be a professional painter, earning her living by her artistic talent.

On her father's side she has an impressive artistic heritage. Tony Snowdon is one of the world's five leading photographers and is nephew of Oliver Messel, distinguished theatrical and costume designer and architect.

Sarah's most celebrated ancestor in her paternal lineage was the beautiful Elizabeth Linley. As a singer, and said to have the most perfect voice in Britain, she was painted as St Cecilia by Joshua Reynolds, first President of the Royal Academy where Sarah now studies. But her lovely singing voice was silenced forever to the public by her husband Richard Brinsley Sheridan, the dramatist, with whom she eloped in 1773. He would only allow her to sing to himself and a small group of friends or when commanded by the Prince of Wales, later King George IV, who included them in his court circle.

The Reynolds picture of Elizabeth was exhibited at the Royal Academy's exhibition in 1775 and proclaimed one of his masterpieces. Joshua's nephew, Samuel Johnson, described the sitter in glowing terms, 'I cannot suppose there was ever a greater beauty in the world, nor even Helen or Cleopatra could have exceeded her.'

Elizabeth, daughter of Thomas Linley of Bath, came from a talented family whose genes have reappeared through the centuries to produce artistic Linley offspring. A visitor to 'the

Sarah helps welcome another royal cousin at the christening of Lady Davina Windsor. She follows the baby's grandmother, Princess Alice, through the grounds of Barnwell, Northants.

nest of nightingales', as Dr Burney described their home, asked the youngest son Tom, 'Are you musical too, my little man?' 'Oh yes,' said Tom, 'we are all geniuses!'

Linley Sambourne, the cartoonist, was a turn-of-the-century relative whose work links him more directly with Sarah, his great-great-grandchild. He excelled at drawing and she, according to Norman Adams, RA, Keeper of the Royal Academy School, is strongest in her charcoal drawings. Sarah has been more fortunate than her ancestor in that there has been the opportunity for a thorough grounding in all aspects of her career.

Linley Sambourne was apprenticed to a firm of marine engineers at the age of fifteen and continued in that job until some of his freelance drawings were accepted by *Punch* magazine. He deputized for Sir John Tenniel, then first cartoonist, for some years and succeeded him when he retired in 1901.

Linley was particularly noted for the great care he took with his drawings, scrupulously observing details of dress and background. He was said by du Maurier to be the only artist in London who could draw a top hat correctly.

Writer Elizabeth Aclin notes in her book *The Aesthetic Movement* that the cartoonist worked 'almost entirely from imagination, producing what were described as quaint and fanciful drawings with captions so brief that the editors of *Punch* provided explanations for their less quick-witted readers.' Sambourne also illustrated some of the novels of the day. Among them were *The Water Babies* by Charles Kingsley in 1885; *The Four Georges* by Thackeray, 1894; and *The Real Adventures of Robinson Crusoe* in 1893.

Linley and his wife Marion had a daughter, Maud, who also became an artist. She contributed drawings to *Punch* and *The Pall Mall Magazine* and married, in 1898, Lieutenant Colonel Leonard Charles Randolph Messel of Nymans in Sussex.

They had three children of which one, Oliver, inherited the great artistic talent of his grandfather. His sister Anne, now Countess of Rosse, was first married to Ronald Armstrong-

Left: *Sarah seldom attends Ascot with the rest of the family because it is simply not her scene, but she turned up in 1986 wearing a very informal pale-blue dress and large brimmed hat.*

Right: *Sarah loves painting flowers, and there were plenty to study at the Chelsea Flower Show, which she attended with the Queen and Princess Margaret.*

Jones and their son Antony married Princess Margaret and became the father of David and Sarah.

With such an artistic legacy their parents steadily encouraged the reappearance of such talents in both their children. The Queen also played an important part in inspiring all the young Windsor siblings in their formative years by showing them the royal treasures and explaining their history. Sarah, her brother and cousins, were able to study and absorb the wonders of the Gainsborough paintings of George III's children; the expressions on their own faces not unlike those of their ancestors on the willow-green walls of the Long Gallery in Windsor Castle.

They all knew the story, and will doubtless tell their children, of how the Queen and Princess Margaret as children slept in the Castle cellars during the war. Around them were the valuable paintings from the Royal Collection that had not been sent for storage in the Welsh mountains.

For Sarah, who has always loved drawings, studying examples of Holbein and Leonardo da Vinci, now in the Royal Library, made her childhood a magical time. Later, when her father took her to Venice and made her get up at dawn so that she could see the glorious city without tourists, she went back and looked at the royal Canalettos through eyes even more aware of their beauty.

The Queen's remarkable collection, dating from the Renaissance to the present day, has always been an inspiration to Sarah who may, one day, contribute paintings herself if her work continues to improve and mature.

As she grew up, Sarah went out on expeditions with the other family painters: The Duke of Edinburgh, Prince Charles and Prince Andrew. She and Charles are particularly *simpatico* and Sarah accompanies him on private painting trips to Italy. She has also begun to teach her brother David some of the joy she finds in watercolours. Her steady boyfriend, Daniel Chatto, is an enthusiastic amateur and it has given their relationship an extra dimension to have this shared interest.

When Sarah left school she had a taste of her mother's birthright when she accompanied Princess Margaret to Canada. But the unblinking spotlight angled relentlessly on the stars of a royal tour were not for a girl who, at that time, preferred the rather scruffy gear of a student and is still completely realistic and down to earth.

'We don glad rags and get on the stage,' said one member of the current royal family with deadly accuracy. None of them could really see Sarah doing that, either convincingly or happily – hence Princess Margaret's decision, after talks with the Queen and Lord Snowdon, to encourage Sarah's flight from 'the royal cage'.

Sarah went first to Camberwell School of Art where she arrived for work in jeans and sweater and mixed well with the other students. At that time she thought of going into the design side of theatre production and sought help and advice from her father's friend Carl Toms, the National Theatre designer. He helped Lord Snowdon with the setting for the Prince of Wales's investiture and has decorated rooms at Kensington Palace and the cottage at Nymans.

After Camberwell Sarah had a year's sabbatical travelling with her father to India as his photographic assistant on the set of 'A Passage to India', and then spent a few months as general help and dogsbody in producer Richard Goodwin's Rotherhithe studio.

She is very close to her father and they have worked together frequently. One of Sarah's jobs was to pose with a doll in her arms when Tony was practising shots for the official pictures after the birth of Prince William. But when it came to taking photographs of his own daughter, to be issued on her twenty-first birthday, the experienced photographer felt self-conscious and unsure. So he assembled a full team – which he really did not need – with lighting assistants, and make-up artist. He and Sarah both immediately relaxed and became totally professional over the assignment. The result was a fabulous picture of a young woman on the threshold of adult life.

Sarah then signed up for three years at Middlesex Polytechnic studying for a BA degree in textiles and fashion. Her years at trendy Middlesex were no sinecure as competition was fierce and her work had to be regularly assessed. 'Sarah had to really study hard to keep up the required standard,' said one of her teachers.

She built up a circle of friends at college – all young and creative like herself, and she also mixed with her brother's Chelsea set. Her first boyfriend was Gerard Gaggionato, an art gallery assistant from Monaco. Friends described him as 'a hot-blooded Latin who pursued Sarah ardently'. The story goes that he then met cousin Helen Windsor whose blonde good looks immediately appealed to him, so he started chasing another demi-royal. The result was a decided rift in relationships between the cousins which was soon patched up when Gaggionato moved on elsewhere, much to everyone's relief.

Then Sarah met Piers Lea, son of a judge. As was not unnatural, Princess Margaret is said to have breathed a sigh of relief and confided to the Queen that this was more the thing. He was not quite up to the Guards officer sprigs of nobility of her own young days, but decidedly better than 'that Italian'.

Sarah loves Italy and is always going there to paint. So when her brother introduced her to Lorenzo Camerana she gave friendship with him a brief whirl until worry about Princess Margaret's lung operation meant she spent more time with her mother.

Cosmo Fry, a childhood friend whose marriage to Lady Cosima Vane-Tempest ended in divorce was said to be very much in love with Sarah and she with him. She used to weekend with a party of friends at his fifteenth-century home in Somerset, and often popped into the local Inn where Cosmo was a member of the darts team. 'Sometimes he and Sarah threw arrows for a bit of fun,' said the landlord Hugh Morgan.

After the romance with Cosmo broke up, Sarah was lonely and occasionally went out on the town with Helen. One night, it was reported, they turned up at Tramps. A club official asked, 'How come we don't see you here more often?' According to him, Sarah replied, 'Unfortunately I do not have an escort to take me out. No one wants to date me because of who I am.'

Happily those days are long past. She now has a steady boyfriend in Daniel Chatto whom she took her mother to see in his latest film 'Little Dorrit'. The Princess enjoyed the first half but it was a six-hour epic and she did not return for the second half.

By Daniel's side, Sarah is fast becoming a true Londoner, discovering places none of the family on the royal side has hitherto known. She is sometimes seen cycling to the Royal Hospital Park, Chelsea, where she helps her boyfriend exercise his two spaniels.

One summer evening they took a picnic supper with champagne to Marble Hill Park in Richmond and sat cross-legged on the grass listening to a musical recital. On another occasion, Sarah – who loves country and blues music – went with Daniel to Harlesden, a suburb of London, to hear Texan Lyle Lovett. They found him in an establishment called 'The Mean Fiddler'. 'Say, do you come from these parts?' Lovett asked the Queen's niece. Then he offered her his latest album. 'I've already got it,' said Sarah.

Nearer home she is an enthusiastic supporter of the Royal Academy's jazz band which played at a private view of the 1988 Summer Exhibition where Sarah was one of the exhibitors. She is now a student at the Royal Academy school – one of nineteen chosen from 300. They have 'exceptional ability' even to get on the short list before they are accepted. Competition for the courses is extremely tough and Sarah has embarked on one that lasts three years. The sympathetic environment is believed to ease the transition from student to working artist. At the end of it a post graduate diploma, equivalent to a Master of Arts degree, is awarded.

'Sarah is a serious painter. She wants to make a career of it,' said Norman Adams, RA, Keeper of the School. 'She is best on charcoal drawings and must work hard on colour where she is weakest.'

For someone who shuns the limelight – she will only brave the paparazzi to help her brother at one of his parties – Sarah has found a quiet working oasis at the Royal Academy. Outside in Piccadilly and above in the galleries, the crowds teem, but the students work peacefully in large, well-lit studios built into the gardens of Burlington House. There is a purpose-built life room where two models pose every day for drawings and paintings. Sarah often works until well into the evening finishing a project.

Over 75,000 students have passed through the Academy School, which was founded in 1768 by King George III, and it is the oldest art school in England. Former pupils include Turner, Constable, Millais, Rossetti, Flaxman, Banks, Gilbert and, more recently, William

Sarah and the Princess of Wales at Smith's Lawn, Windsor.

Right: *Family Christmas. Sarah with Princess Margaret and her cousin Prince Edward leave St George's Chapel, Windsor, after the traditional Christmas Day service.*

Scott, John Hoyland, Paul Huxley and Anthony Caro.

Sarah cycles to school, which takes fifteen minutes from her home in South Kensington shared with a girl friend Katherine Blisher who she first met at Bedales. She has a lodger in the basement flat of the house which was bought with a trust fund set up at her birth by Princess Margaret and Lord Snowdon for both children. The flat is currently being occupied by singing student Dominic West and his rent helps augment the small allowance Sarah gets from her father.

Sarah is a very private person and the Royal Academy staff say she is 'rather quiet'. 'Sarah gets on well with people here,' said Laura Scott, Administrator of the School. 'She really does work very seriously at being a figurative painter who specializes in still life.' Sarah has produced work good enough to be hung in the Summer Exhibition two years running. Fay Ballard, the RA spokeswoman, pointed out, 'Her pictures were submitted anonymously to the Selection Committee like all the other artists' work. They were chosen purely on merit.' In 1987 Sarah showed an oil painting, a still life with green dish; in 1988, two pictures of flowers, one in charcoal and another in water colours of anemones in a glass jar. Like royal paintings exhibited in the past, they were not for sale.

Sarah's friendship with the Princess of Wales began when she was a schoolgirl of sixteen and was asked to be Diana's chief bridesmaid. Her far-from-easy brief was to control the small children who accompanied the bride down the aisle of St Paul's Cathedral. Fortunately she had already had some experience as bridesmaid to Princess Anne when she was only eleven, and so she proved a competent and attractive bridesmaid.

Now that they are both young women, they are even closer. Sarah is a regular visitor to the Wales's home across two courtyards from her mother's at Kensington Palace. She enjoys trying on her friend's new clothes and sometimes gets a royal hand-me-down. Diana is generous in this way, as sisters and friends know. Both Diana and Sarah love dancing and when they are at Balmoral they have been known to stay on at the Ghillie's Ball when the rest of the Royal Family discreetly depart, and then often enjoy a late night snack in the kitchen.

With her brown hair, wide generous mouth and her father's tip-tilted nose, Sarah will never have the great beauty of her mother at the same age. But she has a radiance which lights up her face, especially when she is with someone she loves. Recently Diana has been giving her some beauty tips to add to those she learnt from professional make-up artists on film sets on which she has worked. One that was useful was Diana's trick of using Evian water spray to fresh her face in hot climates or in a warm atmosphere at a public engagement. Sarah found it helpful on the Far East trip she made with her mother and brother. Unlike Diana she can get away with no make-up most of the time. But a little moisturiser is helpful to keep that fine Windsor skin supple.

Like Diana she uses Barbara Daly's colourings from The Body Shop which are applied with an artist's eye for special occasions, usually with her mother who likes her to wear make-up. Barbara Daly did Diana's face for her wedding and advised the chief bridesmaid on a little delicate make-up suitable for a sixteen-year-old. She has remained a friend ever since.

Sarah goes barelegged unless it is very cold when she might wear coloured or white tights. At an evening drinks party, which she usually avoids but will turn out to support her brother, such as the time he launched his china and glass range for Mappin and Webb, she is likely to come straight from school in simple navy suit with no make-up or jewellery.

Sarah likes the country, particularly somewhere she can paint wild flowers. But she is equally at home in London where she sometimes walks up Piccadilly with David and grabs a paper-cup of coffee off a stall. She often shops in Berwick Street market for fruit and vegetables or slips through Burlington Arcade to lunch with cousin Helen in a bistro off Bond Street.

Like her brother, Sarah is especially close to her grandmother, the Queen Mother, who is a famous art lover and collector. She has amassed a glorious, small – by royal standards – collection of her own. It is of particular interest to Sarah because most of the pictures are modern. Queen Elizabeth spotted Lowry long before he became collectable, and has a Matthew Smith, Augustus John and examples of Sickert and Sargent.

Both Princess Margaret's children play the piano but it is their mother who is the star performer. Like all children they went through a phase of feeling embarrassed when she sat down at a piano in one of the royal homes. With a cigarette in a long holder, never far away, the Princess loves playing and singing from musicals with family and guests joining in the chorus. Now David and Sarah are adults with homes of their own, they are more tolerant and join in happily with the others.

When Sarah is staying in one of the Queen's homes she curtsies to her aunt first thing in the morning and when she says 'good-night'. She calls the Queen 'Aunt Lilibet', although at home when talking to their mother both she and David refer to the Queen just as 'Lilibet'.

The Queen knows how interested Sarah is in everything to do with the Royal Collection and keeps her up to date with any new acquisitions. She feels that, as her art training develops, there is always something she can learn from her ancestors' collection.

'Painting is an escape for the Royal Family,' said the Queen's cousin Lady Elizabeth Anson. It has certainly proved so for Sarah.

Not Just a Royal Raver

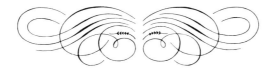

If Queen Mary, that indomitable royal matriarch, could come back for a day to survey the lives of her great-grandchildren and great-grand-daughter-in-law, she would most certainly derive considerable interest from all their careers. And probably be horror-struck by their free-and-easy, liberated lives.

But the job that would really fascinate her belongs to Lady Helen Windsor, twenty-five, daughter of the Duke and Duchess of Kent. She is the descendant most unlike Queen Mary in temperament and attitude to life, whose descriptive nickname 'Melons' – a tribute to her shapely form – would have had King George V's Consort reaching for the smelling salts. But there is a more than passing facial resemblance to her regal ancestor. An old painting show, china-blue eyes and a rounded attractive face, very like the comely Helen.

By the time May – as she was known – was being considered as a royal bride, that lovely hair, the colour of ripe corn, had been fashionably crimped into a frizzy fringe which reminded her future mother-in-law, Queen Alexandra, of a poodle. Queen Mary liked it, however, and never altered it. In time, along with the toque hats and string upon string of pearls, it became as much part of her style as the umbrella with which she prodded her husband when he swore – which was frequently.

Helen Windsor's job in the London art world – she works currently in a gallery in Central London – would have greatly interested Queen Mary as most of her free time was spent combing art galleries and auction houses. Antique shops, particularly in King's Lynn near Sandringham, were a great interest. She also knew the main dealers in London – the world Helen knows so well – and visited them frequently.

Queen Mary was an inveterate collector and re-arranged and added to the royal treasures both at Buckingham Palace and Windsor Castle. Museum directors used to dread her visits because she had no compunction about requesting items she considered should be in the Royal Collections 'on permanent loan'. But, in return, her royal patronage was invaluable and, where possible, she always helped exhibitions by sending an appropriate item from among the royal treasures.

Helen has inherited her love of art and antiquities more directly from her grandparents – George and Marina, the late Duke and Duchess of Kent. They filled their home, Coppins near Iver, Buckinghamshire, with beautiful objects, many of which had to be sold after the Duke's death on wartime active service.

Like all the Kents, Helen loves tennis and is an above-average player. She usually accompanies her mother and father, President of the All-England Club, to the finals of Wimbledon week.

Helen has grown up with reminders of 'that dazzling pair', as they were described in the early days of their marriage by Chips Channon. As Jane Roberts points out in *Royal Artists*, 'George, Duke of Kent was keenly interested in art and formed a notable collection of paintings and furniture. When he married Princess Marina of Greece he reintroduced into the British Royal Family some of the active Continental interest in art that had been so apparent in the nineteenth century.'

Marina's father, Prince Nicholas, was a talented painter who sold work to augment his income when the family were in exile in Paris. Two of his paintings hang in Windsor Castle and others in the homes of the Duke and Duchess of Kent and Prince and Princess Michael of Kent.

Marina studied art in Paris – just as her grand-daughter Helen was to do after leaving school – and became a skilled portraitist. Her likeness of the late Cecil Beaton was 'a hundred times better than I expected,' he said.

George was greatly influenced by his mother Queen Mary's love of collecting, and Sir Oliver Millar, until recently Keeper of the Queen's pictures, called him 'the most distinguished royal connoisseur since George IV'. So it is not surprising that Helen Marina Lucy Windsor, born a bouncing baby of 7 pounds 8 ounces late on the spring evening of 28 April 1964, was to grow up with similar interests. She was the third of the royal quartet to arrive after her cousins Prince Edward and James Ogilvy and three days before one of her future best friends and cousin Sarah Armstrong-Jones.

The Queen had a luncheon party at Windsor Castle before her christening which most of the Royal Family, including her godparents Princess Margaret and the Hon. Angus Ogilvy, attended. The baby was named after both grandmothers and her beautiful Romanov great-grandmother the Grand Duchess Helen Vladimirovna, who married Prince Nicholas of Greece wearing the fabulous pink diamond first worn by Catherine the Great of Russia and, afterwards, by all the Romanov brides.

The girl who was to grow up nicknamed 'The Royal Raver', was a placid, happy child with a sunny disposition. Most of that good nature remains even today when she has to endure more than is fair of gossipy stories in the tabloids. 'It's true she is pretty lively and likes a good time but most of the reports are totally blown up,' said a Kent family friend. 'Helen is used to it now and tries not to read the stories.'

It would not be unnatural if Helen developed an aversion to the paparazzi who tend to follow her around. She does try to avoid being photographed because it makes life easier for her in her job but when it is someone known she is unfailingly courteous. Once she met a bunch of photographers at Sandringham and she posed smilingly for them, helpfully tossing back long dark-blonde hair which was partly hiding her face, and chatting away as the photographers worked.

Helen is one of the fortunate among royal women – the Princess of Wales is, of course the prime example – who always photographs well. Like Diana she is glossy and glamorous with an interesting sense of style. She is an expert skier, tennis player and water skier – 'Terrific at most sports,' said a friend.

The Kents prefer a quiet private life and when their children were growing up they tried to give them a world far away from press cameras. At that time the Duke of Kent was in the army, mostly stationed abroad. After her birth, Helen and her elder brother George were absorbed into the busy life of a military barracks in Germany.

It was soon after Helen's christening that the Duchess took their then family of two – a younger boy Nicholas was born in 1970 – to rejoin her husband with his regiment, the Royal Scots Greys. Their home was in Quebec Avenue, Fallingbostel, a four-bedroomed house built for British officers with standard-issue furniture and a tiny garden which was just big enough for the baby's pram and playpen.

Helen was almost eighteen months when they left Germany and returned to Coppins. They celebrated the homecoming by, amongst other things, a nursery tea-party when their children got re-acquainted with their cousins Prince Andrew, then six, and Prince Edward, whose godmother was the Duchess of Kent. Helen and Edward got on famously together and it turned out to be the first of many playtimes. For with the rest of the quartet they grew up sharing outings, parties and holidays until they were twenty one when the Queen gave them a splendid ball at Windsor Castle.

Aunt 'Lilibet' was especially interested in Helen's progress because she was so near Edward in age. Their spring birthdays reminded the Queen of the epic Christmas at Sandringham in 1963 when there were four expectant royal mothers: Princess Margaret, the Duchess of Kent, Princess Alexandra and herself. It was the first time, someone recalled, since George III's reign when four of his daughters-in-law were all pregnant together, that there had been such a prolific year. At Christmas luncheon the toast was, 'All the little strangers whom we know are present.'

When it was decided to sell Coppins, the country house inherited from Princess Victoria, sister of King George V, the Queen gave the Kent family a grace-and-favour apartment in St James's Palace. York House was the first married home of George V and Queen Mary and later it was taken over by her eldest son, the Prince of Wales, later Duke of Windsor. He completely refurbished the old rooms which he described as 'a rambling, antiquated structure, a veritable rabbit warren with passages interrupted by unexpected flights of steps leading to unsymmetrical rooms full of ugly furniture.' The Prince was helped in the restoration by his brother Prince George, later Duke of Kent, who, if he could have foreseen the future, would find his elder son and family installed there.

An antique lamp hangs above the front door of York House; the old clock in the rose-red tower still chimes the hours above busy St James's Street, and guardsmen stand sentinel outside the entrances to this ancient palace. They are all part of Helen's background, along with the quiet house the Queen has loaned the Kents in the country – Anmer Hall on the Sandringham Estate.

Spending their holidays at Anmer, Helen and her brothers learnt the ways of the Norfolk countryside. 'Dear old Sandringham,' wrote their great grandfather George V, 'the place I love better than anywhere in the world.'

From the Hall it was a walk or a bicycle ride to join cousin Edward and, usually, Sarah Armstrong-Jones, during the school holidays, and with them Helen explored the fenlands. There were adventures sailing on the Broads and happy days spent on the golden sands of a Norfolk beach. The Queen still keeps a small house on the dunes from where the family swim and picnic.

Helen's schooling was very conventional except for her sixth form days which she spent in a tough co-educational school in the Highlands. She went first to St Paul's School for Girls in London and then on to St Mary's, Wantage, where her cousin David Linley's future girlfriend Susannah Constantine was also a pupil. By the time Helen was sixteen, Gordonstoun School, where her cousins Charles and Andrew had been pupils, and Edward was just entering the Sixth form, had become co-educational. Sarah had told her cousin about her own co-ed school, Bedales, and Edward, who loved Gordonstoun as Andrew did, said, 'Why not come?'

The Duke and Duchess, always forward thinking and enlightened, clearly thought it would do Helen good to mix with boys of her own age. So off she went to the tough school on Scotland's Moray Firth. It had a spartan image and life there followed the fresh-air principles of Kurt Hahn, Headmaster to the Duke of Edinburgh as a boy.

As a bouncy extrovert Helen took to Gordonstoun just as her cousins Andrew and Edward had. Charles did not like it but it was arguably the wrong school for his temperament. In the Prince of Wales's day, conditions were really exacting and included two cold showers a day and a punishing schedule of outdoor activities. But with the advent of girls, and by the time Helen arrived, the tempo had noticeably eased. After all, who cared about wearing shorts – which inevitably froze the lower legs in those northern climes and were a great source of complaint – if the girls were wearing them too?

Of course some stories filtered out of Gordonstoun about the dishy blonde sixth-former. One pupil who was there at the time, said, 'Melons was one of the most popular girls. Though she wasn't the most beautiful she was certainly one of the sexiest.' She was much appreciated for jogging round the playing fields in tiny shorts. And when she went off to sunbathe with the other girls, the boys who owned binoculars became suddenly popular.

Here then, in the person of a sapphire-eyed blonde teenager who looked a bit like Queen Mary as a girl, was the spice in the 1960s' batch of young royals. It is said her high spirits may have put a silver thread or two in her mother's head for a time.

Newspapers called her 'a sensational royal rebel' but then, as Mandy Rice-Davies might say, they would. When she sunbathed topless in Corfu with her boy-friend John Benson, a stockbroker's son, it made headlines. But Helen was not doing anything more unusual than anyone else of her age on a holiday beach. It is doubtful, however, whether the ancestors on grandmother Princess Marina's side would have approved of their scantily-clothed, but

Above: *Helen is an expert ski-er, tennis-player and water ski-er. 'Terrific at most sports', said a friend. She is pictured during a family ski-ing holiday in France.*

A special night out at Covent Garden. Lady Helen Windsor accompanies her parents to the Queen's 60th birthday gala concert.

very pretty descendant – particularly as the Greek Royal Family's Summer Palace is on Corfu, although there are only royal ghosts there now, since King Constantine and his family went into exile in Britain.

Then Helen wandered on to the balcony of Buckingham Palace to watch a fly-past after the Trooping the Colour ceremony. She looked very fetching in her summery outfit but she carried a glass in her hand and actually raised it to her lips. It caused twitches among the 'old guard' and another black mark. It was just a thoughtless action by an inexperienced youngster who had forgotten the form. But it earned her more criticism.

Helen continued to break some rules with her colourful social and love life. She has had several boyfriends, but her parents have been extremely sensible in letting her have her 'head' and they have not been let down. Helen's brother George introduced her to her first boyfriend John Benson, an old school friend. Whilst he was at Edinburgh University he earned some money by running a mobile discotheque called 'Raffles'. She went ski-ing with him and he joined the Kent family in a holiday to Corfu where the famous topless sunbathing incident took place.

The next boyfriend was another old Etonian, Nigel Oakes, a record producer. Like her mother who sings in the Bach choir, Helen has a suberb singing voice and Nigel gave her a recording test. He would have liked to make her a star but the embargo came down on that one. 'There is no way she could make a record,' said Nigel, 'which is a shame. She has a wonderful voice – very natural, uncomplicated and not forced. But she wouldn't dream of cashing in on her royal connections.'

Nigel himself was soon on the embargo list. Helen had smuggled him into York House one night and breached strict royal security. 'An irate Duke of Kent banned him from visiting the house for some time,' said a friend.

Somewhere in between these affairs, Helen had a brief fling with her cousin Sarah's boyfriend Gerard Gaggionato which, for the first time in their lives, caused friction between the two girls. Helen herself dismissed the rumours as nonsense.

Helen's love affair with David Flintwood, an advertising executive, lasted several years but it is believed to be over now. He is a quiet, serious young man whose personality appeals to Helen in that incomprehensible – to others – attraction of opposites. She is dashing, bubbly and unconservative about most things. He may be quiet but is strong and dynamic, and she does listen to him.

David certainly helped Helen over a great trauma in her young life which affected her greatly: the death of her friend Olivia Channing of a drugs overdose and the jailing of Rosie Johnson, an old schoolfriend from St Mary's, for drugs offences.

The Kents must have been fearful, as all parents of youngsters would be, that their vulnerable daughter had been so close to tragic friends such as these. But there is a backbone of good common sense about Helen Windsor which has got her over bad patches in the past. When her mother was ill with severe depression after the loss of a baby, which would have been her fourth child, Helen was a tremendous source of help and encouragement. She gave up her job to be with the Duchess, acting as companion and temporary lady-in-waiting: helping to ease the passage back to a normal working life.

One of her best traits is carefree optimism, both hopeful and revitalizing to anyone with whom she comes into contact. Like her mother she is a caring and very understanding person when anyone is in trouble. The Queen is said to be very fond of this young cousin, appreciating that she was a good and compassionate daughter when most needed by her mother.

The family are all aware that beneath the light-hearted approach to life is a serious young woman, fascinated by her career and who aims to make a success of it. With her A level in Art from Gordonstoun Helen went to Paris for a spell and continued her art studies, as her grandmother Marina had done in the twenties. Then Helen went to Christie's, the auctioneers, as a receptionist, meeting members of the public who wanted someone to tell them if the family heirloom had any worth. With her knowledge from childhood of the royal treasures, her instinctive flair and artistic background, Helen found she had a keen eye for a fake. She was promoted to the Contemporary Art Department which interested her cousin Sarah with whom she queued for lunchtime sandwiches in a Mayfair bar. The pair – known to friends as 'the lady-birds' – often meet for lunch and a chat. Again it is the attraction of opposites: Sarah Armstrong-Jones is quiet and dark; Helen volatile and fair.

After Christie's in London she went to New York for a spell to work in their office there

Right: *Lady Helen Windsor and her mother, the Duchess of Kent, are very close. When the Duchess suffered ill-health after a miscarriage, Helen gave up her job to be with her mother, acting as companion and temporary lady-in-waiting until the Duchess felt better.*

Above: *Helen worked for a time at Christie's the auctioneers, both in London and New York. She is seen attending a charity auction at Christie's in 1987.*

Right: *Helen missed her family when she went to New York to work. Here, she and her father, the Duke of Kent, with most of the Royal Family, attend the wedding of James Ogilvy.*

as a trainee. It was a great adventure and Helen was very excited about it. But in that noisy, stimulating city Helen had no roots. She became quieter than usual and lonely. Obviously her job in New York 'as part of the company's total learning experience' was all a little too much.

'She's a little subdued – probably because she's overwhelmed with all the new names and faces,' said Roberta Maneker, Christie's spokeswoman in America. It was an unusual description of the vivacious Helen and had her London friends puzzled. She missed her boyfriend David, who popped over as often as he could to see the New York working girl, but most of all she wanted her family and London, the city she knew so well. Another problem was the cost of living in the Big Apple. Although Helen used a Christie's company flat, which saved her paying rent, her salary of around £15,000 a year did not go far. Living in the Del Monico building in Park Avenue she was surrounded by expensive temptations.

After spending Christmas in Britain with the Royal Family, she resigned from Christie's on New Year's Eve, but decided to stay on in America to join the 'visual arts foundation' set up by the Trustees of the Andy Warhol estate. Then there was difficulty over renewing her work permit, so Helen came home to start a new job working for the modern art gallery Karsten Schubert in Central London.

She lives in a flat near Victoria Station, not far from Buckingham Palace, and commutes to work by car or underground. Sometimes she walks through St James's Park, listening to music on her 'Walkman', on her way to see her parents at York House.

Helen and Arabella Cobbold, with whom she shares the flat, love nightclubbing, and often sally forth with their boyfriends several evenings a week. But they are both up bright and early to arrive punctually at their jobs.

'Helen is quite ambitious. If she wants something she goes out and gets it,' said a friend. 'She is actually an innocent in a wolf's clothing – not nearly as naughty as the rumours would have us believe.'

Sarah Armstrong-Jones sometimes joins her cousin on shopping trips – often for the chunky modern jewellery that Helen likes so much. Her love of flamboyant fake earrings and necklaces would not have been approved by her great-great-grandmother, the Grand Duchess Vladimir of Russia. She had a magnificent collection of jewellery, said to be second only to that of her mother-in-law the Dowager Empress Marie Feodorovna, according to Leslie Field in her book *The Queen's Jewels*. The Grand Duchess left part of it to her daughter Princess Nicholas, mother of Helen's grandmother Princess Marina, who in turn bequeathed some pieces to her daughter-in-law, the present Duchess of Kent.

Helen is likely to inherit some of her mother's jewellery one day, among it a few of the Romanov treasures. But, unfortunately, most of the best pieces had to be sold when Prince and Princess Nicholas were in exile. One of the most magnificent – a diamond and drop-pearl tiara which the Queen often wears – was smuggled out of Russia by a young Englishman. He disguised himself as a woman and hid the tiara in his bonnet, according to the late Countess of Airlie.

She was the grandmother of Sir Angus Ogilvy, Princess Alexandra's husband, and faithful lady-in-waiting for many years to Queen Mary. The tiara was bought from Princess Nicholas by King George V and it became one of the Queen's favourites when she inherited it on Queen Mary's death.

However, owning valuable jewellery is certain to be far from Helen's mind as she enjoys her life as a lively bachelor girl around London, although as an art connoisseur it is natural she should be interested in the colourful stories attached to the jewellery once worn by her Russian ancestors.

In their day Helen would have been safely married by now; part of the great dynastic chain that linked European royal families. Queen Victoria liked her close royal relatives, particularly on the distaff side, to marry royalty before their twenty first birthdays. But Helen's future – and that of her cousins – is very different. Like them she has been allowed to live and love comparatively freely. This independent life-style is looked on tolerantly by the Queen, so conservative herself, but inclined to be easy-going with those of her family not too close to the throne.

If – and when – Helen marries, she will wear a treasured piece of Valenciennes lace, part of the wedding dress of her great-grandmother and namesake, the Grand Duchess Helen, which was the 'something borrowed' in both her grandmother's and mother's wedding dresses.

It may help to bring good fortune to the Queen's sparkling young cousin with Imperial Russian blood in her veins.

Lady Helen Windsor and Lady Sarah Armstrong-Jones are great chums as well as cousins. Friends in the young royal circle call them 'the lady-birds'.

7

Stan

George, Earl of St Andrews, heir to the Dukedom of Kent, has always kept in the background of the media spotlight that plays on other members of the Royal Family. He said firmly at the age of nineteen, 'I have managed to remain anonymous so far in life and I want to stay that way.'

But somewhere the fates must have been wryly smiling, for quiet, studious 'Georgie', who never went to wild parties like his sister Helen or fell foul of the speeding laws like his Linley cousin, only six years later was to inspire considerable publicity for such an unknown royal. He was to incur the Queen's minor displeasure and forfeit his place in the succession to the throne, by his engagement and subsequent marriage to a Roman Catholic divorcee, Sylvana Tomaselli.

But when George was born at 3 pm on the afternoon of 26 June 1962, at 'Coppins', the Kent home at Iver, Buckinghamshire, a future so royally unconventional was far from his family's thoughts as they gathered to welcome him into the world.

Earlier, his grandmother, the beautiful Princess Marina, the widowed Duchess of Kent, had summoned his aunt Princess Alexandra to the house. 'Come at once,' she said. 'Kate is starting to have her baby and she needs all her family with her.'

It was an indication of just how close the Queen's Kent cousins are within their own immediate family circle. But in Buckingham Palace, also, both the Queen and Prince Philip, who two years ago had started their second family with the birth of Prince Andrew, were eagerly awaiting the news.

The 6 pounds 4 ounces infant was duly welcomed in an appropriate way for a June baby whose great-grandfather had ruled a country whose national emblem is the rose. The members of Iver Women's Institute had the happy idea of each picking the choicest bloom from their garden to send a very personal bouquet of June roses to the young Katherine Duchess of Kent on the birth of her son.

Her husband 'Eddy', the Queen's soldier first cousin, was a keen photographer and, like Prince Andrew was to do twenty-six years later, took photographs of his Duchess and her child soon after he was born.

Such was the interest in the village that George's pram was wheeled outside the gates of 'Coppins' by Scots nanny Mary McPherson, so that the small crowd could have a glimpse of the infant Duke.

George St Andrews hated parties and the grand life of the court when he was growing up. The formality and protocol surrounding the Queen were sometimes an ordeal for the shy youngster.

At his christening on 14 September, the usual ritual of all Queen Victoria's main descendants was followed. The gold lily font came from Windsor Castle and the fragile Honiton lace christening robe – last used by his cousins Andrew in 1960 and David Linley in 1961 – was carefully unpacked from its layers of black tissue paper to clothe the new young Windsor. The Archbishop of Canterbury officiated at the ceremony and most of the Royal Family gathered in Buckingham Palace to 'wet' the baby's head.

He was christened George after his great-grandfather King George V and his grandfather the late Duke of Kent who died in a wartime air crash; Philip after his godfather, the Duke of Edinburgh, and Nicholas after his other great-grandfather, Prince Nicholas of Greece.

It was at his christening that someone said how 'angelic' he looked. His blond, blue-eyed looks continued to justify this description throughout his childhood and schooldays, much to his chagrin. Friends say this was why he grew the beard, 'and certainly no one could call him "angelic" with that,' said one.

The Queen, the Queen Mother, Princess Margaret and Princess Alexandra – his god-mother – were among other members of the Royal Family who paid young 'Georgie' the supreme compliment of forsaking the normally sacrosant Scottish holiday at Balmoral to attend.

George was then tenth in Succession to the throne. But, as a princely title ends with the children and grandchildren of the Sovereign, he was the first future Duke of Kent not to have the prefix H.R.H. before his name. But this baby's ancestry was very royal indeed. Like all the Kents and the Ogilvy children he is descended from both Romanovs and Hanoverians. Two great Queens, Catherine of Russia and Victoria of Britain, are ancestors. Their royal blood mingled with that of six European royal houses. Princess Marina, his grandmother was always very conscious of her family's heritage and wanted her children to marry into other royal families – which none of them did. 'Breeding will out,' was one of her maxims.

The Queen's attitude towards marriages of the younger royals is that she would prefer direct descendants to keep the line as aristocratic as possible. The alliance of Charles and Diana is one such marriage, for the Spencers are a great old British family.

After his christening, apart from a few appearances as a page at weddings, George St Andrews appeared to vanish from the royal scene. But actually he was very much there – just keeping quietly in the background, unless pushed to the front at, for instance, a Palace review of a fly-past after Trooping the Colour which he watched with other nursery-age royals at the edge of the balcony.

Soon after George's birth, the Duke was posted as second-in-command to a Squadron of the Royal Scots Greys, based in Hong Kong. The Duchess and her baby son joined him there when he was nearly six months old. They travelled in a troop-charter transport aeroplane with other army families and the Duchess remembers changing George's nappies and feeding him in the cramped corner allotted to them.

It was also a tight squeeze for the family and Nanny McPherson in the small army flat in Barbecue Gardens, Castle Peak. As the Duchess mentioned in a letter to Princess Marina, it was all rather different to her elegant home in Kensington Palace, where they had recently been staying. But they were very happy in Hong Kong. Between George and his mother, who was then able to spend much of her time with him, there developed the devoted bond that was so apparent as he grew older.

Nanny McPherson found she had ample time to explore Hong Kong while the Duchess wheeled her baby in his pram to a local park most afternoons. The Chinese were fascinated with the flaxen-haired small boy and called him 'the little one with winged knees' because at ten months he was such a speedy crawler, according to reports at the time. The family amah was also delighted and forecast great good fortune as his first birthday was on the fifth day of the fifth moon and coincided with a Dragon Boat Festival.

When George was fifteen months the Kents returned to Britain and he was plunged into the heart of the many royal family Christmastides he would attend in future. It was the year notable for four heavily pregnant royal ladies. The Queen was expecting in March; Princess Margaret in May; the Duchess of Kent in late April and Princess Alexandra at the end of February.

In the nursery the Earl of St Andrews was introduced to Prince Andrew, then nearly three, and Viscount Linley, two. But unlike his sister, who grew up very close to the others in the 1964 quartet of royal births that was to come, George never really had much in common with the other two, except cousinship.

From the start he was exceptionally bright and clever, taking after his grandfather and namesake whom George V always said was the most intelligent of the children. Unlike Andrew and David, who had lessons in Buckingham Palace, George went to the local school and had music and movement classes with the village children. He has always been fond of music and the Duchess encouraged this by lessons in piano and drums which he loved.

George was two when his sister, another blonde baby like their mother, was born.

Soon after, the family went to Germany on another posting where they renewed acquaintance with the large net of European royal cousins in various countries.

Some time after they returned to 'Coppins', George joined Andrew at Heatherdown Preparatory School in Berkshire and it was while he was there that the Royal Family were badly shaken to hear of an apparent IRA plot to kidnap Andrew. The Prince had, by this time, left to go on to Gordonstoun, but his younger cousin was still protected by the security set up for him.

The Duke and Duchess of Kent were, however, still alarmed and it was said to be one of the reasons for selling much-loved 'Coppins' and moving to houses on royal property, easier to protect in the event of security problems.

'Coppins' had been left to the late Duke of Kent by Princess Victoria and, at first sight, the rambling, multi-gabled Victorian house did not seem a suitable setting for such an elegant pair as Marina and George. But they painted it cream outside with green shutters, transformed the interior into a comfortable but fashionable home, and filled it with treasures collected or inherited – Fabergé, Tsarist silver and antique fans.

After Eddy married, Marina, now Dowager Duchess of Kent – although she preferred the title Princess – vacated the house to live in Kensington Palace. Her son and his wife kept the family home much as it had been and they all loved it. When the Queen then offered them an apartment in St James's Palace, York House, and the lease of Amner Hall on the Sandringham Estate as their country home, the final move from Buckinghamshire was made, much to the sadness of the Iver villagers.

At Heatherdown George was showing the early academic skills which were to earn him the nickname 'brainbox' from his less gifted cousins. He won a King's Scholarship to Eton – where his father and uncle had been pupils – at the age of twelve, competing with seventy-six other candidates for one of only fifteen scholarships. In a stiff set of exams George came eighth in all subjects, and, already showing his talent for languages, first in French.

His scholarship came just a year after it had been obvious that cousin David Linley would not even get through the entrance examinations to Eton. But David, as he has since proved, was to have equally good but different skills, and will probably earn more material benefits from his work than his more intellectual, less street-wise cousin.

The Headmaster of Heatherdown was naturally delighted and proclaimed a half holiday for everyone. The Queen was also happy when she heard the news as she knew how much this would mean in terms of hard cash to George's parents. It was also true that she felt some pride in his achievement.

As Elizabeth Longford observes in *Elizabeth II*, 'everything that the cousins do counts, in the sense that they too are part of the extended Royal Family. When one of them wins a scholarship it is one up to the Monarchy. When another gets divorced it may be one down.' It could be said, perhaps, that in winning a scholarship and marrying a divorced woman the Earl of St Andrews has balanced the scales.

His time at Eton was marked by his growing interest in books and learning. He, himself, thought of the nickname 'Stan', abbreviated from his title, probably because, as an old school friend remarked, 'He was sick of some boys calling him "Georgie-Porgie".'

Throughout his years at Eton, with his royal ancestry always there in the background, however anonymous he tried to be, the outline of Windsor Castle was only a cycle ride away. When the other boys went cheerily home for the Christmas holidays, George's reunion was always clouded by the knowledge that in a few days he would be in the formal surroundings like 'Dickens in a Cartier setting', as the late Duke of Windsor once described a royal Christmas.

'He hated parties and social life,' said a relative of the Queen. 'His parents wanted him to go to grand parties the Queen gave but he really couldn't cope.'

Christmas wasn't so bad because the Queen and the Duke always tried to make family holidays informal. And the Kents usually stayed in one of the Towers so they were all together. But it still was not George's scene and, as the years went on, it became less so.

He was expected to do well in his A level exams but he disappointed tutors and family by failing two of three subjects. It was unfortunate that the exams coincided with a time when his home life was shadowed by his mother's ill-health. He adored her and was naturally greatly troubled by her condition of acute depression following the loss of a baby. A few months later, after some intensive study, he re-sat the exams and came out with top grades in History, English and French.

When at Eton, George had been extremely interested in his cousin Anne's accounts of her travels for the Save the Children Fund. He has inherited his mother's caring nature and when he left school asked if he could help at one of the Fund's base camps.

The Duke and Duchess of Kent at St James's Palace on their 25th wedding anniversary. Two years later their eldest son was married in a registry office – very different to their own glittering wedding in York Minster.

Travelling under the name George Andrews he worked for four months in India for the Fund and the Boys Town Trust. He became so interested in the country and its complexities that he read Sanskrit – the ancient and sacred language of the Hindus – with Social Anthropology as post-graduate courses at Cambridge. He followed his cousin the Prince of Wales to the university in 1981 and graduated with a 2.2 degree in History. He then decided to stay on to complete the post-graduate courses.

In the library at Cambridge he met an attractive, dark-haired Research Fellow in History, four years older than himself, with whom he fell instantly and passionately in love.

Sylvana Tomaselli was a Canadian divorcee who had recently been co-editor of a book of essays on the subject of rape. She was not the usual 'donnish' academic but an elegant dresser with a low, beautifully modulated voice who, like George, enjoyed long intellectual conversations.

For them both, that meeting in the tranquillity of a university library was to be a memorable one and would eventually make Sylvana a member of the Royal Family. At that time she was a quiet, reflective woman who had been through a sad experience with her unsuccessful marriage, and she lived for her work.

George, like his cousin Charles, was already a man who thought deeply. Intelligent and sensitive he was inclined to be almost reclusive. Sylvana, also a quiet private person, found an immediate empathy with this tall, blond young man who, until he knew her intimately, talked little about his background.

He ex-husband, John Paul Jones, who probably knows her better than most, talks without rancour of their time together, simply acknowledging that she was not for him. He described Sylvana as 'one of the most serious people I have ever known. She is an intellectual and I'm the sporty type; she likes to have fun but a meaningful, intellectual discussion is more stimulating for her.'

When George began his studies at Cambridge he bought a small end-of-terrace house in Victoria Park. Some time after their meeting Sylvana moved in with him and they lived there blissfully happy and busy with their work for eighteen months.

George's parents were worried about their love affair on three counts: the four-year difference in their ages was one factor but the over-riding problems were Sylvana's religion and divorce. The Duke and Duchess, quite naturally, had no wish to upset the Queen or the Archbishop of Canterbury, one of whose predecessors had married them and christened George. But they are a loving family and were gradually won over as their son quietly but with great firmness maintained his love for Sylvana, insisting, 'She is the only one for me.'

If he had been a different personality they might have counselled patience. But it was not easy to forget that Princess Marina had urged this on them with the resulting long delay in their marriage. The Queen was saddened by her young cousin marrying a divorcee and a Roman Catholic, but, like everyone else in the family, appreciated that an eligible girl of average brain, however attractive, was not for the future Duke of Kent.

'He needed someone whose intellectual capacity equals or exceeds his own,' said a relative. 'I believe they are extremely happy together. She is rather beautiful, which is a considerable bonus.'

The Queen granted her permission, which is necessary under the Royal Marriage Act, observing rather sorrowfully that it was the second time in a decade that a Kent cousin had forfeited his rights to the Succession. Ten years earlier Prince Michael of Kent had renounced his place to marry Marie Christine von Reibnitz, another Roman Catholic divorcee. The beautiful, sometimes controversial, Princess Michael has two children, Lord Frederick Windsor, born 6 April 1979, and Lady Gabriella Windsor, born 23 April 1981, who have taken their father's place in the Succession.

George and Sylvana's engagement was announced on 10 June 1987 – by coincidence the birthday of his godfather, The Duke of Edinburgh. The couple moved for a spell into the limelight, posing for photographs in the grounds of stately Lancaster House, and Sylvana showed off her beautiful sapphire and diamond engagement ring.

The small house in Cambridge, where they had been so happy, lay empty that day. On the doorstep was a note for the milkman cancelling future deliveries, and another rather poignant note accompanied a bouquet of flowers from a father to a much-loved daughter on her engagement day. 'Best wishes and good luck, Papa', it read.

Sylvana and George had a celebration lunch with his parents and sister at York House and met other members of the Royal Family later in the day.

Knowing her son's dislike of formal parties, the Duchess arranged another happy, very relaxed celebration at Sandringham, three miles from Anmer, a week before their wedding. She picked a night when there was a full moon and borrowed the Queen's log cabin – very popular with the younger royals – as the setting for a rather special barbecue. In this informal atmosphere members of the Royal Family, at Sandringham for the New Year break, toasted George and Sylvana's future happiness. They ate charcoal-grilled steaks by the light of the moon and a huge bonfire, and it all went off beautifully, as the Duchess had planned.

The next day, after the church service at Sandringham, Sylvana, who had naturally been rather nervous of meeting her distinguished future in-laws en masse, could be seen having a lively talk with the Prince of Wales and Princess Anne.

Of all the Queen's family, Charles could be expected to appreciate her rational, scholarly outlook on life. But, for the holiday, it seemed Sylvana had forgotten her books.

'She was positively glowing and obviously very much in love,' said a Kent family friend. 'She is a charming girl.'

The Royal Marriage Act of 1772, set up by George III, somewhat unjustly dominated their wedding plans. Under its stipulations the couple were barred from a registry office ceremony in England or Wales. Nor could they be married in church as the Act does not sanction a member of the Royal Family marrying a Roman Catholic. Also Sylvana had been divorced, which makes even a normal church wedding difficult.

Scotland was the obvious choice and Leith Town Hall became the somewhat unlikely venue for a royal wedding on 9 January 1988. Sylvana's father, Austrian-born Mr Max Tomaselli, was there to give the bride away in Britain's first civil royal wedding. George paid £24 for the ceremony which included the purchase of a marriage certificate which cost £2. But in a gesture towards his royal birth, perhaps, the registrar delivered the papers personally to Holyrood Palace, the Queen's residence in Edinburgh where George and his family were staying.

Mist from the North Sea edged into the port where Mary Queen of Scots first stepped on to the soil of her Kingdom of Scotland. And a thousand people deemed the event of enough romantic interest to turn out on a cold winter's day to watch the proceedings outside the Town Hall.

There were echoes of the bridegroom's Russian ancestry in the bride's Cossack-style, vivid blue satin hat; more than a hint of another, more elegant age, in the cut of her extremely stylish royal-blue suit with its matching muff. Or, perhaps, the colour could more correctly be called Cambridge blue to honour their university.

Sylvana carried a bouquet of white flowers, interspersed with lucky white heather, tied with blue tartan ribbon. She wore a sapphire and diamond brooch and earrings, a present from her bridegroom, to match her engagement ring. There had obviously been some collaboration on George's wedding outfit – his tie exactly matched the bride's suit.

Top: *At Leith Registry Office a thousand people turned out on a cold day to watch the proceedings at the Town Hall.*

Above left: *The Earl of St Andrews at Sandringham just before his wedding, with the Princess Royal and Captain Mark Phillips.*

Right: *George and his bride Sylvana had to be married in a Scottish registry office because she was both Roman Catholic and divorced.*

Prince and Princess Michael of Kent were also affected by her religion and previous marriage. Their civil wedding in Vienna was followed by a religious blessing at Westminster Cathedral some years later.

As the Act expressly rules out the wedding of an heir to the throne – however remote – to a Roman Catholic, and the Queen is Head of the Church of England, it was not possible for her to attend the wedding. Nor, for the same reason, could the Duke of Edinburgh, who had sponsored George at his christening. But his godmother Princess Alexandra was there to preserve the link with that first ceremony.

It was all very different to the grand religious occasion in Buckingham Palace twenty-five years before. In spite of this, those of his family gathered in the port of Leith that gloomy winter day were heartened to see how happy George was with his bride. His parents heard them exchange their civil vows, together with Lady Helen Windsor and Lord Nicholas Windsor, his sister and brother. And his uncle Prince Michael of Kent with his wife, Marie Christine, who knew so well all the background to George's renouncement of his right to Succession, were also there to support him. As were his aunt Princess Alexandra and her husband, Angus Ogilvy, with their son James.

The Queen was absent but her unseen presence lent substance to this family event. She allowed them to use the Palace of Holyrood House for their wedding reception, and in other kindly ways welcomed Sylvana as George's wife to the family.

Her Majesty also gave permission for a service of blessing in St James's Chapel. Still, she did not attend, but the Queen Mother, the Princess of Wales, Prince Edward, the Duke and Duchess of Gloucester, Princess Alice of Gloucester and most of the Kent family were present to celebrate the religious blessing of the marriage.

Afterwards George and Sylvana packed up the house in Cambridge, and that period of their lives, to start another chapter. George had decided that a career in the Diplomatic Service might satisfy his inbred wish to be of service to the Crown and his cousin the Queen. It would also give him, he hoped, the discreet anonymity he wanted from life and the opportunity to use his undoubted gift for languages.

As a start – even before he sat his Foreign Office exams – it was arranged for him to embark on a six-month tour as Third Secretary in the British Embassy in Budapest, Hungary. For Sylvana, torn from her Cambridge libraries and research outlets in the middle of work on a new historical book, it was something of a change in life-style.

First they had a honeymoon in a castle in Germany, lent by a relative. 'She did feel at first that she was being sent into exile,' said a university friend. They drove 989 miles to Budapest in their Ford Escort. 'Thought it would be a nice way of seeing Europe,' said George laconically. It was also the only reasonable way of transporting all the research material Sylvana needed for her book.

She is currently working on The Enlightenment – 'more particularly the Scottish and French Enlightenment', she wrote from Budapest. 'The eighteenth century has been my main area of publication so far and I hope to be able to pursue my research here as elsewhere.' The study of an eighteenth-century philosophical movement which stressed the importance of reason and critically reappraised existing ideas and social institutions, is a major new step in her academic career and means lengthy research.

Sylvana had plenty of time to work in the small flat in Budapest after seeing George off to the Embassy each morning. His work, described by spokesman Jonathan Stoneman, was to meet Hungarians and write political reports for his Ambassador. 'He'll also have lessons in Hungarian during his stay.'

Sylvana thought Budapest 'spectacular' and she and George enjoyed it all tremendously. Known as 'The Paris of the East', the two cities of Buda and Pest were a splendid place to start married life for a young royal. Few people knew who they were and soon they were making friends with Hungarians who were, as Sylvana put it, 'Most friendly and open with us. We have met some very interesting people and have enjoyed our stay here immensely.'

According to Jonathan Stoneman, 'Budapest is one of the most interesting ports in Europe – interesting but not too tricky for someone with George's origins. We have very good relations with the Hungarians but somewhere like Moscow might be more sensitive.' There lies the nub of the matter. George, a fluent Russian speaker, will never be able to work in Moscow, unless there are very radical changes, because his great-grandmother Princess Nicholas was a member of the Russian Imperial Family.

He is the first of the British Royal Family to earn his living behind the Iron Curtain and no one is more interested in his diplomatic experiences there than the Queen. It is not everyday she can talk to a Third Secretary who is, moreover, her cousin.

'I suppose it might seem a bit incongruous for me to be behind the Iron Curtain,' commented George. 'But nobody here thinks so. They address me as it comes. Sometimes it's Mr Andrews; sometimes it's Lord St Andrews.'

In the homeland of Liszt, Lehar and Bartók, he and Sylvana enjoyed their anonymity. They dined out to the strains of romantic gypsy music in some of the capital's many restaurants, explored the city – claimed to be the greenest in Europe – with its many parks and woods and visited the museums and theatres.

Although it is a Communist country, Budapest is full of life and colour. The late Queen Mary, George's great-grandmother, used to say it was her Hungarian blood that gave her such an appreciation of vivid colour. Through Queen Mary, George – like his cousins – is descended from the Hungarian Countess Claudine Rhedy who was morganatically married to the royal Duke Alexander of Wurttemberg. Her son Francis, Duke of Teck, was Queen Mary's father.

If he passes his Foreign Office exams, George St Andrews, his wife and baby son, born just before Christmas 1988, will embark on life in the Diplomatic Service which these days is very much about trade with other countries. Entertainment and 'feeling the pulse of the country' will be part of the job, and George, with Sylvana's help, is certain to get over his dislike of parties just as some others in his family have done. But whether he will ever be an unknown royal again is doubtful.

8

Jo and Mo

The younger generation of the Queen's family have made an effective debut in their chosen careers but they have, to some extent, been moderately sheltered by their student or professional status.

Not so the Ogilvy pair James and Marina, children of the Queen's first cousin Princess Alexandra of Kent and her husband Sir Angus Ogilvy. James and Marina have already seen more of the world outside privileged palace circles than their cousins, although they have all experienced life uncushioned by the protection that accompanied their younger days spent in royal homes.

But James and Marina began much earlier. In their teens they met the challenge of earning a living head-on – because they wanted to be self-sufficient. James took a job on a factory assembly line and house-painting; Marina worked as a shop girl in London's West End and, later, became an instructress to drop-out youngsters from the city's East End.

They go behind the scenes that older members of the Royal Family see only from the outside and their experiences have made a remarkable impression on their lives, however humdrum they may be in the future.

James Ogilvy, born in the thirteenth hour of 29 February 1964, was a 9 pounds, 6 ounces Leap Year baby who was, moreover, thirteenth in line to the throne until his cousin Prince Edward arrived ten days later. His parents joked about it at the time as their gardener and his wife with other members of the staff toasted the baby's future.

He was to grow up lively and enterprising – 'a Jack of all Trades', as one of his future employers described him. The first of the quartet to arrive during that productive royal baby year, James would be the one brimming with dynamism and with the will to tackle anything.

The Imperial blood of Catherine the Great of Russia and the less fiery Hanoverian did not course sluggishly through his veins. James has, so far, always been a doer with some of the impetuous energy of his aristocratic Ogilvy forbears, famous as gallant fighters; the first in Scotland resolutely to champion a cause.

The Queen, who had always been especially fond of 'Alex' (or 'Pud' as she was known to the family), agreed to be her baby's sponsor at his christening and has taken a great interest in his progress ever since. The Duchess of Kent, his aunt-in-law, Prince Michael, his uncle, and the late Sir Robert Menzies, the Prime Minister of Australia and an old friend of the Princess, were the other god-parents.

The Ogilvy pair: 'Jo' and 'Mo' with their parents, Princess Alexandra of Kent and the Hon. Angus Ogilvy, attend a family wedding.

He was baptized James Robert Bruce, sturdy Ogilvy family names – with no hint of Romanov, Hanover or Windsor, but possibly in salute to the Scots King whom his ancestors followed into battle. Nevertheless, his demi-royal status was recognizable by the Victorian christening robe – which was brought out of storage to start a busy year – and the gold font from which the Archbishop of Canterbury poured the Jordan waters on to the young Ogilvy. He was the first baby to be christened in the chapel at Buckingham Palace since it was badly bombed during the war. By coincidence, his mother, Princess Alexandra, granddaughter of George V, had been the last.

Just as his great-grandmother Mabell, Lady Airlie, had devoted much of her life to the Royal Family as lady-in-waiting and confidante of Queen Mary, James grew up as the close friend of the cousin nearest to him in age – Prince Edward. Because of the bond between them he is likely to stay close also to the two girls in the quartet who are slightly younger, Sarah Armstrong-Jones and Helen Windsor.

Of the four, all great-grandchildren of King George V, James is the only one without a title, because, although his mother is a Princess of the Blood Royal, his father is the younger son of an Earl who ranked only as an Honourable until he was knighted in the 1989 New Year's Honours. As the first untitled man to wed a British Princess, he was the example that helped Captain Mark Phillips stand firm about not accepting a title when he married Princess Anne. It means that the Queen's first two grandchildren, Peter and Zara Phillips, are untitled. Viscount Linley and Lady Sarah Armstrong-Jones have their titles because their father, photographer Antony Armstrong-Jones, became Earl of Snowdon on his marriage to Princess Margaret from whom he was subsequently divorced. Ironically his second wife, Lucy, is of course a Countess and their daughter is Lady Frances Armstrong-Jones, but neither are connected in any way to the Royal Family.

Although James is interested in music, art and photography, as they all are, his working life-style is very different to other royals in his age-group. He has elected to join the tough, stimulating life of the City – the 'square mile' dominated by the Bank of England, Stock Exchange and Lloyds, now extending its boundaries deeper into the river docklands. No other member of the Royal Family has been 'something in the City', apart from Prince Michael of Kent at director level, but there is a recent tradition that the men of the Ogilvy family work there. James's grandfather, father and uncle all joined City firms and held directorships in others. James, himself, is now a trainee in a large investment bank.

At present Angus Ogilvy holds directorships in Sotheby's, the Rank Organization and the Metropolitan Estate and Property Corporation. He had many more in the past but association with the Lonrho company, which was censured for breaking trade sanctions with Rhodesia, forced him to resign most of them. He now devotes much of his life to charity, particularly raising money to help unemployed youngsters in the Inner Cities. His other interests include helping to create jobs in the Youth Business Initiative, Youth Clubs UK, Arthritis Care and the Carr Gomme Society which aids people with drug, drink or related problems.

Nothing about James's childhood would have prepared him for the cut-and-thrust of a computerized dealing floor. It would seem a million miles away from the quiet schoolroom in Buckingham Palace where he learnt his first sums with Edward and Sarah under the guidance of 'Mispy' – 'Miss Peebles' – who had once taught his mother.

On the large globe in the schoolroom they followed their parents' journeys if they were away, and James felt the first stirrings of an urge to travel which would become one of his consuming interests.

He went home to Thatched House Lodge in Richmond Park each day to a nursery where, it is believed, General Eisenhower worked out plans for the D-Day landings when the house was taken over by the American army during the last stages of the war.

James and his sister Marina, who is two years younger, had a marvellous childhood in the old house, once a keeper's lodge in the royal hunting ground. They rode their ponies over the green acres of Crown land, and played and picnicked in the thatched summer house in the garden. As they grew up they gave each other nicknames which they found usefully informal as they went out into the world – first to boarding schools and then jobs. James was 'Jo' and Marina was 'Mo', after their initials.

James went to Gibbs preparatory school with Edward and then on to Heatherdown, but from there their paths diverged. He joined his Kent first-cousin George, two years his senior, at Eton, where in his father's old school he did well academically, leaving with thirteen O Levels and three A Levels. He also won the photography prize which gave him the confidence to take an official picture of his parents, sister and himself which was released before one of Princess Alexandra's official tours abroad.

That the Ogilvy streak of adventure had rubbed off on James, soon became apparent as he took his first confident steps into the working world.

In his late teens he was handsome, as he is now, with none of the gangling awkwardness common at that age. James has the classical good looks of his mother but tempered by some of the rugged, craggy mien of his father's side of the family. He also has the vigorous Ogilvy approach to life which propelled him into earning his living as fast as possible. This led to a variety of jobs which gave him an entirely new comprehension of the world outside 'the eiderdown' of a royal home, as a member of the Queen's Household once described the cocoon-like effect of over protection.

He worked as a navvy in a bottle-making plant, mixing easily with his workmates and joining them for a beer after work in the local pub. He drove a lorry and became an electrician for interior designer Nicholas Haslam, who said, 'We all muck in here. James is a "Jack of all Trades". He changes plugs, does re-wiring, even some painting and van driving. It is a purely professional thing. He gets the rate for the job.' He also worked as an assistant to photographer Sir Geoffrey Shackerley who several years later took his wedding photographs.

James's father would have smiled to himself when his son came home to tell of his working life. Angus Ogilvy had been through similar experiences himself as a ship's cabin boy, waiter at the Savoy, cattle rancher in Rhodesia and office boy in the City.

The Queen, his godmother, was amused and interested to hear of James's latest endeavours. To his cousins of the same age – Edward, Sarah and Helen – he lived in a different world which they longed to join. In time, of course, they did, as the concept of royals taking ordinary jobs grew more likely with each one that broke the mould.

James, at seventeen, was already showing business initiative. He hit on the idea of publishing a give-away, glossy magazine for Londoners called *Freeway* which he still thinks of nostalgically because, for its brief life, it was a success. He persuaded his father to lend him some money and launched the magazine after 'cold-calling' at business firms all over Central London. With lively charm, he talked his way into the offices of, in most cases, the Managing Directors, and persuaded them to buy space in his magazine.

He had promised his father not to approach any of his City friends or use his name to get special treatment. James only broke this assurance once, by mistake, when he went to see someone he did not realize was a business friend. He found James such a good salesman he bought the back page and rang his father to congratulate him on his son's business acumen.

The loan was paid back after the first two months and the magazine made a small profit. 'At least James's magazine washed its face,' said Angus Ogilvy, who was delighted by his son's achievement but equally determined it would not be his career. 'He is certainly not going to be a newspaper proprietor. He went into a field he knew nothing about and had the luck to do well.'

It is not difficult to understand the reason for the next stage in James's career. After two years in publishing it was time for some square-bashing in the army and a change of scene. He joined his father's old regiment, the Scots Guards, on a short-term commission and was sent to Hong Kong where they were stationed.

It was an old stamping-ground for the Kent family and somewhere they had all loved. James had heard about the Colony from his aunt and uncle, the Duke and Duchess of Kent, who were stationed there when George was a baby, and from his mother who had paid a popular official visit, and his father who had also been stationed there before his marriage.

Like them he visited the floating restaurants by the waterfront, shopped for presents for his family in the bazaars and looked across to the paddy fields of distant China. He visited the Philippines, Borneo, and Malaya, serving in the jungle patrols, just as Angus Ogilvy had done in his day. 'I lived on bananas and coconuts,' he said.

When he finished his tour of duty and knew he did not want to make a career of the army like his uncles 'Eddy' and Michael, James wrote home to say he would be working his way back to Britain. He took several jobs in various countries before starting four years reading History of Art at St Andrew's University, Scotland.

He had digs in the home of Peter Erskine at Cambro near Crail, where everything was free and easy and comfortably relaxed. James enjoyed his stay with the Erskines and described it as 'a fun palace where everyone gets the most out of life'. But, true to form, he worked his way – baby-sitting the couple's four children and daily stoking their boiler.

It was not too far to go to spend weekends with his uncle and aunt, Lord and Lady

At a crowded London party just after their engagement was announced, James and Julia have eyes only for each other.

Beautiful Julia Rawlinson experienced the warm welcome of everyone in the Royal Family.

Airlie, at Airlie Castle, the family seat and his father's ancestral home. There he renewed acquaintance with the legend of the family ghosts, which happily did not appear. One of them is the Airlie drummer whose drum roll is said to precede the death of an Earl of Airlie. The other is a chill feeling of extreme fear, which James's great-grandmother described in her memoirs. The late Sir John Colville, who was for many years the Queen's Private Secretary and a most rational person, spoke of a terror 'impossible to describe' which he felt at Airlie. But to everyone's relief there have been no reports of either presence in recent years.

At Scotland's oldest university, founded in 1410, James tried to resurrect his brainchild *Freeway*, but his college base was too far away from London to sell advertising. He concentrated on his hobby of photography in spare time from studies. As he also has the royal quartet's shared artistic flair, he was always being asked to design sets, paint posters and act as creative adviser for the university's drama productions. He plays the piano well, like all the Kents, and was in demand to perform after quiet dinners or rowdier, beer-bashing student parties.

On the same course was beautiful Julia Rawlinson, who became unpopular at first with James's rumbustuous friends because he was so diverted by her undoubted attractions. 'We weren't terribly thrilled with Julia – but she certainly made a lasting impression on him,' said one of James's college friends. 'Julia was always coming up with little treats. For his twenty-third birthday she took him to Venice. We couldn't compete with that.'

James, at that time, was always short of money and Julia had a rather more generous allowance. Neither Princess Alexandra nor her husband could afford to give him more –

and it is doubtful if they would have done anyway, believing their son's money-earning efforts were character-building. So he always worked in the 'vac', becoming 'really good at house-painting,' said a relative.

That accomplishment should come in useful as a young married man. For Julia had indeed made an unforgettable impact on James. They came south with degrees at the end of the course, and both took jobs in London after three months holiday in California together. James started as a trainee with the investment bank, Barclays de Zoete Wedd, and Julia did some 'temping' and then got a job, like Sarah Ferguson before her, with a Public Relations firm.

They shared a flat and James told his parents he wanted to marry Julia. Princess Alexandra, fearing that twenty-three was on the young side, cautioned them to wait. 'She thinks they're too young to get married and approves of the idea of them living together first,' said a friend.

The Queen was naturally interested in the love affair and asked James to bring Julia to Balmoral so that she could meet her in person. The Queen Mother invited the young couple to Birkhall where James's parents had spent their honeymoon, and they spoke of their hopes of marriage.

James, like George St Andrews who also wanted to get married at this time, had to get the Queen's permission even though, by now, he was way down the line of Succession. But, in his case, there were no problems of religion or divorce and the way was clear for a traditional church wedding with most of the Royal Family in attendance. But before that, James travelled to Edinburgh, a city he knew well from his student days, to support his cousin George at his small, quiet registry office wedding to Sylvana. He knew already, as he stood beside his parents for the family wedding photographs, that he would be the next of the generation to marry. It was to be a very much grander wedding than that of his cousin but it is doubtful whether each young couple felt very different on their wedding days, despite the contrast in circumstance.

James celebrates with some of his friends.

James and Julia took part in several family events that spring and summer and Julia experienced the warm welcome of everyone in the Royal Family. They joined Princess Margaret and Lady Sarah Armstrong-Jones when cousin David Linley launched his new range of china and glass at Mappin and Webb. As they admired his work they were probably looking at his wedding present to them, as he always likes to give his own creations.

Fifteen members of the Royal Family, headed by his godmother the Queen, travelled to Saffron Walden in Essex to see James marry Julia on 30 July 1988. It was clear from their beaming smiles and obvious approval that there were no royal doubts about this wedding. The Queen, delighted that her godson was so happy, thoroughly enjoyed his nuptials and, as Princess Alexandra said afterwards, 'It was such a beautiful wedding and a marvellous occasion.'

The three still single members of the quartet, Edward, Sarah and Helen, who had shared most of the important days of his life – like their joint twenty-first birthday party given by the Queen at Windsor Castle – were in the pews of St Mary the Virgin Church to see James wed.

Among the 400 guests was the Royal Family contingent led by the Queen, the Princess of Wales, Princess Margaret, Viscount Linley, Lady Sarah Armstrong-Jones, the Duke and Duchess of Kent, Prince and Princess Michael of Kent, their son Lord Frederick Windsor and daughter Lady Gabriella (Ella) Windsor, who was a bridesmaid, and the Duke and Duchess of Gloucester.

Princess Alexandra, elegant as always, held on tightly to her husband's hand as the couple exchanged their vows. His sister Marina's eyes were bright with tears as she watched her stunning new sister-in-law sweep the Queen a deep curtsy as they left the church.

Minutes earlier trumpeters of the 17/21st Lancers, of which Princess Alexandra is Colonel-in-Chief, sounded a fanfare as the bride and groom with the Queen and their parents appeared after signing the register.

For his sister Marina life at home in Thatched House Lodge would never really be the same again without James as her close confidant and companion.

Marina was born on 31 July 1966, and was royally received into the world with the names Marina (after her grandmother Princess Marina), Victoria (after her great-great-great-grandmother Queen Victoria), and Alexandra (after her mother and great-great-grandmother Queen Alexandra). Now she is grown-up she uses her nickname 'Mo' which allows her the anonymity which, like cousin George, she aims to preserve.

Prince Charles was one of her godfathers and has been a great friend and support ever since. They share the same love of solitary Highland places, disinterest in extravagant society parties and the urge to make other people's lives more stable and worthwhile.

As she was two years younger than the others there was no royal of the same age to share her schooling, but Marina eventually followed cousin Helen Windsor to St Mary's Convent School, Wantage, and left in 1984 without any scholastic achievements like A Levels.

Marina's path lay in a very different direction to university. She, too, had inherited the adventurous streak of the Ogilvys and was soon to realize it. Marina had heard all about 'Operation Raleigh' from her godfather who had helped to set it up. But it was not until she was lying in a hospital bed after an appendicitis operation, that she identified herself with the round-the-world adventure journey for young people. There was a poster on the wall advertising 'Raleigh' and, as Marina looked at it, she thought, 'Why not?'

'I was depressed and feeling at a low ebb,' she said later. 'Operation Raleigh was a challenge to me to get back.'

When she left hospital Marina said nothing to Prince Charles or her parents. 'I didn't

Fifteen members of the Royal Family travelled to Saffron Walden, Essex, to see James Ogilvy marry Julia Rawlinson on 30 July 1988.

A friend thought Marina occasionally looked a little sad at her brother's wedding. 'But then all her lovely, bubbly personality took over and she was herself again.'

want to be accepted for the scheme because of my family,' she said. 'I wanted to do it entirely on my own.' She wrote, giving her school address, and was selected for an 'assessment weekend' which organizer Duncan Walpole said was 'extremely tough'.

'We put them through hell for the whole weekend,' he said. Everyone thought highly of Marina who was, said Walpole, 'a good sort.' But then came this perceptive remark, 'In a way she's more disadvantaged than a venturer from the East End of London. It's harder for her to fit in as just one of the crowd because of all the limelight she attracts.' Yet the judges who knew her only as 'Miss Ogilvy' must have considered she overcame this handicap well and was ideal material for the adventure of 'Operation Raleigh'.

Duncan Walpole was looking rather more deeply beneath the surface at the problem which gnaws away at all the young royals. How can they be normal when they are the constant prey of paparazzi cameras? Asked whether she was worried about sharks when she was diving in the Caribbean, Marina replied promptly, 'I'm more worried about little boats of photographers following me.'

Prince Charles was immensely proud of his goddaughter when she took up the gauntlet of a project very dear to his heart. But, for Marina, there was a not inconsiderable problem to tackle first. She needed £2,800 for the trip and was determined to raise it herself.

'I had no intention of asking my parents,' she said at the time. So she went to a Job Centre, as her brother had done, and they found her work in Harvey Nichols, one of the Princess of Wales's favourite stores. 'I enjoyed it and might go back,' said Marina. 'The pay was quite good.'

Marina shuns the limelight and seldom attends public events. One of the few was with her parents, at a celebrity shoot in North Wales. Also in the picture are the Princess Royal and her husband Mark Phillips, the Duke of Kent and ex-King Constantine and Queen Anne-Marie of Greece.

But she only managed to save £10 a week towards her project. This gave her less than she needed but she was allowed to write ten letters asking for sponsorship. There must have been one or two VIPs who helped, but all Marina would say was, 'People were very kind.'

She chose the scuba diving mission on Roatan Island, 120 miles off the coast of Honduras. She had only previously dived on holiday but 'Raleigh' trained her at RAF Gulford, Wiltshire, where they worked twelve-hour days. 'Six hours in the pool and several lectures every day,' said Marina. There were thirty divers working on the community project, usually in a fierce wind in cold lagoon waters. They made records for marine surveys, observed plant and animal life and dived to explore sunken galleys. Another job was to blast a channel through the reef to help islanders.

Marina said goodbye to her parents and set off on a charter flight to South America with a laden 70-pounds rucksack. Her equipment included a diving mask, snorkle, flippers, fishing gear and a few waterproof clothes, bikinis, shorts and tops.

Letters home were few and far between because they were so busy, but Marina tried to tell her family some of the excitement she felt when she explored a sunken wreck, helped build a school for local children in the jungle and restored an old lighthouse. She also made a lot of very good friends from walks of life she could never have known in the normal course of events. 'They're very supportive and kind, and great fun. They take me as a person rather than for anything else – like who my mother is,' said Marina.

To writer Douglas Keay, who flew out to interview her for *Woman's Own* magazine, she said frankly, 'I'm not a rebel but I felt I wanted to make my own friends, rather than be pushed into being an upper-class sort of girl.

'Talking to others I'm so envious that when they come home from school their parents were always there. My dear old parents were always being called away because of their jobs.

'Before "Operation Raleigh" I felt trapped and very low. A year before, I had peritonitis and was anorexic for a time. I had become very withdrawn, and though both my parents were very supportive I think they worried about me.'

Marina hoped that her participation in 'Raleigh' would change some people's views of the young royals. 'Personally I don't like the image of racy upper-class kids bumming

Left: *Young Marina with her mother, Princess Alexandra, during the family Christmas at Windsor. Pictures of Marina are rare. 'Life is much easier if people don't recognise me,' she says.*

Above: *Just before this picture was taken on Christmas Day 1982, Marina had spent some days in hospital after overturning her Ford Escort car on a wild mountain road in Wales where she was undergoing an Outward Bound course.*

Left: *Marina is not often seen at smart parties, but here she is on one of her rare sprees – at a party in London, cigarettes in hand.*

around. I find their lives are selfish and false. They haven't done anything or experienced anything worthwhile.'

Her friendships became very valuable. When she returned to Britain, Marina said, 'You don't make friends by going to a succession of parties or by getting drunk and being stupid. You make friends by doing things.'

In 1987, Marina started working for the Drake Fellowship, another of Prince Charles's pet projects which he set up after the success of 'Raleigh'. It was an adventure training scheme for underprivileged children, particularly from the Inner Cities. Marina worked with a team in London helping youngsters who had got into trouble with drugs and crime. She did so well at these 'character-building' courses that she was offered a job at the Outward Bound School in Applecross in Wester Ross where 'concrete jungle' boys and girls are taught how to survive in the rugged mountains of Ross and Cromarty.

It was just the sort of remote Highland country, up a track 2,000 feet high and snowed up in winter, that appealed to Marina. But she had to go through a tough three-month mountaineering course before she qualified. On the way to the Capel Curig Centre on Snowdonia her Ford Escort overturned and she found herself in a Llandudno hospital for two days. But after Christmas at Windsor with the Royal Family, she continued the course, tackling the steep side of the mountain in the roughest of January weather.

In the Highlands, Marina was very happy. It was a spartan job but she loved it so much she cried every time she took some leave. She was known as 'Mo' to everyone and was paid £7,300 a year to instruct youngsters in mountaineering, rock climbing and canoeing in a rugged outdoor life. Marina summed it all up when she said, 'I have come to love this place. But what pleases me most is the effect all this remote beauty has on the Inner City youngsters.

'In the mountains or in a canoe – they mellow. And when they are put in what we call stress situations it brings out the best in them.'

It was the sort of assessment that brings joy to the Prince of Wales's heart. He and Marina are regularly in touch and the Queen is also deeply interested in her work.

At Applecross, Marina's quarters were a room 8 feet by 12 feet. She lived in anoraks, sweaters and climbing boots and daily washed out her thermal underwear in the communal laundry room. Recreation was found in the Applecross Inn – where she celebrated her twenty-first birthday – very different to the Windsor Castle ball given by the Queen for her brother and cousins. Marina like James is also a talented pianist, and used to play in the inn on Saturday and Sunday nights, joining in a sing-song.

She loved the long days on the hills, sometimes four at a stretch. 'Time doesn't matter,' she said. 'At first I used to sleep under canvas. Now I prefer to zip myself up in my bivi bag in the open air. The local people knew who she was in time, but reacted admirably to having one of the Queen's cousins in their midst. 'They have been very protective towards me and this has allowed me to live a normal life,' said Marina.

When Marina came home to Richmond her parents persuaded her to calm down her life-style and do some training that might be useful in the future. She enrolled for a year's diploma course in catering and lived during the week at the small flat the Queen has loaned Princess Alexandra and her husband in St James's Palace.

She is looking at a variety of careers. There was even talk of her joining a pop group, 'The Sweatbands', which was formed by Baroness Isabella van Randwyck and former royal equerry the late Major Hugh Lindsay who died in the avalanche at Klosters when a member of Prince Charles's party.

'As a parent I don't mind what she does so long as it's respectable and Marina is happy. She certainly loves music,' said Angus Ogilvy.

9

'I Play My Part - They Play Theirs'

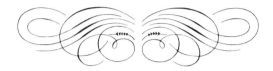

The baby who was to be called 'the theatrical royal' and become the first child of a reigning monarch to take up a full-time job outside the services, was the second of the quartet of royal births in 1964. The Queen has described him as 'the quietest of my children'. Her cousin Lady Elizabeth Anson says he was 'a gentle little thing with a mass of blond hair'.

Prince Edward, the Queen's youngest child born when she was thirty-eight, was a model son conforming to conventional royal standards all along the way until, at the age of twenty-two, he jerked the leading strings and courageously stood his ground against further conditioning in the Royal Marines. A service life was not for him, he told his parents firmly and refused to change his mind in the face of an angry father who also happened to be Captain-General of the Marines.

All his life, until then, Edward had been trying to live up to the standards Prince Philip set his sons. They all had the tough Gordonstoun education, and in the holidays the even tougher instruction in their father's concept of manliness.

Edward did well in both schools and appeared to be as malleable as any princely recruit to the system. But the mistake he made was in not going to university before starting his service career.

'If it had been the other way round he'd have attracted less attention by his decision,' said a relative. 'But now he is so enthusiastic about his theatre job, the fuss is all over and his parents are delighted.'

The end of a difficult year for Edward came in February 1988, when it was announced he had joined Andrew Lloyd Webber's The Really Useful Theatre Company. He knew he would have to start from the bottom and newspapers had great fun calling him the royal tea-boy and dogsbody. But, more factually, Edward was embarking on a challenge every bit as demanding mentally if not physically as his Marine training. Like his cousins he had to prove that he was not doing someone out of a job; that he did possess the flair and talent to be a successful – useful – member of an extremely profitable business.

It had been said that his career in the Marines was not helped by his apparent 'cockiness' and difficulty in mixing with his brother officers. Indeed, the same could be said of Prince Andrew before his Falklands experience, which matured him as an officer and a man. But, if it were true of Edward, it must have been because he and some of his brother officers were temperamentally incompatible. The most striking thing about Edward's life behind-the-scenes at the Palace theatre is the way he has been accepted. From the theatre door-man – no push-over for the famous, he's used to them – who said, 'We really admire him so much for doing what he's done,' to the theatre cat who gets a tickle under the chin and tit-bits from the Prince when he brings back his lunch-time sandwich, Edward has been received with approval.

Edward puts in a long working day – 9 am to often after 7 in the evening. Then, there may be a public engagement on behalf of 'The Firm' back at the other Palace HQ. Or he may take home a script to read and report on its potential.

Andrew Lloyd-Webber, with his hitherto unerring instinct for picking a winner, be it a production or its stars, is on record as saying he was impressed with Prince Edward's enthusiasm and willingness to learn from the lowliest job upwards. He will certainly be getting reports of the Prince's progress as he deals with the sometimes humdrum tasks which lie behind the success of a production.

Edward, as everyone calls him, arrives at the Palace theatre just before 9 am every morning, accompanied by his 'minder' (there is no relief from the Royal Protection watch-dogs, even in theatre-land). In the seedier parts of Soho where Edward moves around in his normal, day-by-day working life, he probably needs the burly, highly trained police officer by his side.

If the Prince is first in, he is quite likely to make the tea. But they usually take it in turns among the six working in the small, busy office. 'We all muck in,' said Edward's boss, Biddie Hayward. 'It's not unknown even for me to make the tea!' He makes a start on the day's work by opening the mail which then goes on to Biddie. He sorts out applications for jobs on one of the Lloyd-Webber shows from bills for current productions. During the morning there may be team meetings, or stars to be dealt with tactfully on the phone.

Edward begins to learn about a royal life of service. There was no reason to suppose then that his future would not follow a conventional royal pattern, like this walkabout at the age of fourteen.

The end of a difficult year for Edward, and the dawning of a theatrical career. He had to start at the bottom, and newspapers had fun calling him 'the royal tea boy'. The Prince joined in the joke by arriving at the appropriately named Palace Theatre carrying a well-known brand of tea-bags.

Edward usually nips out for a sandwich with his detective and queues with others in one of the many bars around the theatre. He has patronized the 'Gulp!' sandwich bar whose owner says of his royal customer, 'He seems very down-to-earth and quite appealing really. No one ever recognizes him when he comes in.'

Sometimes Edward goes to a local fish restaurant or with his work-mates to a Chinese restaurant. On another occasion Andrew Lloyd-Webber took a bunch of them out for a curry at 'The Last Days of the Raj' in Drury Lane. The restaurant owner wanted to put up a sign saying By Appointment to H.R.H. Prince Edward but was told the visit had been strictly private.

In the afternoon he may be chasing props or diplomatically giving the bad news to an actor that he has not been chosen for a show. There are scripts to be collected and sent to the publisher. 'Putting it all together', he calls it, using a phrase not unknown to his sister-in-law Sarah York.

'We all had reservations,' said Biddie Hayward, the company's executive director. 'The fact of who he is will inevitably raise the question of why we're employing him. But that could lead to reverse discrimination. He's bright, he's intelligent and he has made it clear that theatre is not just a passing whim.'

Prince Edward backstage at Covent Garden after a performance by the Russian Opera Company.

Prince Charles was sixteen the year his youngest brother was born and plans for his future preparation as heir to the throne must have been much on the Queen's mind as she bent over the crib, in which she herself had lain, on Edward's christening day. There was no reason to suppose his future would not follow a similar pattern of initiation into a life of service. School, university, the armed forces. Then good works, endless ceremonies and, as the Princess of Wales has observed, 'the constant smell of fresh paint' wherever a royal is expected.

Princes have always gone into the services or, as Prince Philip once suggested, the church. Their only connection with the theatre was as a patron or by dalliance with some footlights beauty.

The late Cecil Beaton, who took the photographs of Edward's christening, may have sensed this baby would be different. The Queen's relaxed attitude to Edward hinted there might be some dispensation for him in the strict royal rules previously followed.

'The infant showed bonhomie and an interest in the activity that was going on,' wrote Beaton in his memoirs. 'His behaviour pleased and amused the Queen who was in a happy, calm and contented mood.'

Beaton had noticed the tranquil way the Queen behaved towards her last-born which was to characterize their whole future relationship. She was even more at ease with this baby than she had been with Andrew – so different to the early days of the elder pair, Charles and Anne. Beaton further noted that the infant Prince was 'alert, curious and already a character'.

'Look his eyelashes are all tangled,' said the Queen, admiring her son. 'It's most unfortunate that all my sons have such long eyelashes while my daughter hasn't any at all.'

As the baby of the family, born on 10 March, soon after his cousin James Ogilvy, he was always given more of her time than the others, mainly because circumstances allowed it. The Queen was very much in command of her job as she had not been when Charles and Anne were in the nursery. She had more free time for her younger family and they benefited from this mother and child bonding.

The new Prince was christened Edward Antony (after his godfather Lord Snowdon), Richard (after the Queen's cousin the Duke of Gloucester), and Louis (after his great-great-grandfather Louis of Hesse).

98

Nurse Mabel (Mamba) Anderson was sympathetic to the Queen's desire to spend as much time as possible with Edward. She used to don a large rubber apron and bathe him each evening, helped by any visiting royal who happened to be there. Once there was one king and three queens in the nursery bathroom, splashing and sailing boats with the latest young Windsor.

Andrew and Edward were allowed to play in the Queen's sitting room while she did her boxes, unheard of in the younger days of her first two who had the door firmly closed on them.

Perhaps the most important factor in Edward's upbringing was the good fortune that produced four royal babies in one year. They played together as toddlers, shared nursery school at Buckingham Palace, and Edward cannot remember school holidays without them for company. They were all gentle, lovable children with none of the dominance of Andrew who always pushed himself forward. They got on extremely well and there were few quarrels and tantrums as there were occasionally between Andrew and David Linley, the nearest to him in age.

Like all the young royals, Prince Edward adores his grandmother. He greets her affectionately at Scrabster Harbonn when the Royal Family visited the Queen Mother at the Castle of Mey.

The old schoolroom at Buckingham Palace was full again, but 'our dear Mispy' as the Queen referred to governess Miss Peebles, sadly died and was replaced by Lavinia Keppel. Her ancestress was Alice Keppel, the mistress for many years of the children's great-great-grandfather King Edward VII.

Although Edward was not as forceful and was sometimes over-shadowed by his elder, more boisterous brother Andrew, they were always friends and remain so today.

Edward is by nature more like a Windsor than a Mountbatten though he has his father's colouring and beaky nose. His is a character of some depth and he has a personality which, like all his family, can be autocratic. But he is sensitive and caring with great determination when he makes up his mind.

Although he is devoted to his brother and future King, Prince Charles, it is his sister Anne whom he loves best. Ever since she came home from Benenden to play with him in the holidays, they have been close. When Edward was growing up, shy and awkward, he spent a lot of time at Gatcombe Park, Anne and Mark's home. He had freedom and informality there and plenty of riding at which he showed the family competence. His mother gave him an Arab mare – a present to her on a Middle East tour – and it always accompanied him to Gatcombe. There Anne helped him with his jumping, and stable-girl Shelley Whitborn used to ride out with him. Edward occasionally dated her in the school holidays.

He found the Phillips's eighteenth-century manor house 'very cosy' and 'home-like', and so it must have been after Buckingham Palace which none of the Queen's family really likes. There were children's toys stacked underneath the stairs in the black-and-white paved hall, dogs curled up in chairs and an easy-going atmosphere with none of the formality of a royal home. Significantly it was to Anne he went after a stiff and somewhat traumatic last meeting with his Marine CO. Edward spent some days trying to relax at Gatcombe before joining his parents at Sandringham.

After the Palace schoolroom he followed the educational pattern of recent royal schoolboys. He and cousin James Ogilvy went to Gibbs Preparatory School in London and then on to Heatherdown which was, by then, well used to royal pupils and the security problems they created.

Heatherdown was conveniently close to Windsor Castle and Edward used to take friends home to tea at week-ends. His birthdays were especially popular as the royal chef used to bake an extra large cake, a slice of which was given to every boy in the school.

After Heatherdown Edward and James separated. James went off to Eton and his cousin followed his father and elder brothers to Gordonstoun. Although Edward's earliest years had promised some easing of the rules worked out by their father for the royal children, there was no immunity from the system during his school years. Character-building was the maxim by which the Duke made men of his boys. And Gordonstoun, scene of his own spartan boy-hood, was where the steel in their backbones was forged. The fact that his daughter, Princess Anne, who never went there, has more than any of them is ironic.

To Gordonstoun they went and the younger two found it a very different place from their father's and elder brother's days. The advent of girls and a new headmaster, John Kempe, had made it a less strict, more relaxed establishment. Andrew, two years senior, was already known as something of a Casanova when his younger brother arrived. Unlike Charles, who hated it, they both thoroughly enjoyed the school, and so did Lady Helen Windsor who spent her sixth form years there.

Edward's school years were interspersed with home life punctuated with royal ceremonies that seemed to gather more media momentum with each one. First there was his sister Anne's wedding in 1973 which turned out to be a royal pageant of spectacular

Edward shares his family's competence at riding and the Queen's love of horses. They are pictured watching the Royal Windsor Horse Show.

Edward and his mother the Queen and his sister-in-law Diana.

dimensions. But the whole production, stage-managed by the Lord Chamberlain, and watched by an estimated 500 million throughout the world, must have paled into insignificance for young Edward when confronted with the 'one-upmanship' of his elder brother Andrew who had been collected from Gordonstoun by an aircraft of the Queen's Flight.

At this time Edward, like most youngsters, was suffering from introverted shyness. To find his tomboy sister transformed into the archetypal princess – suddenly remote in her white bridal gown and tiara – came as something of a surprise. It was swiftly dispelled by her re-emergence as the sister he knew rather better, with all her old matter-of-fact ways, the next time he saw her in the Christmas holidays.

At Anne's wedding, Edward was a page, a situation mitigated by the presence near him in the procession of his cousin and crony Lady Sarah Armstrong-Jones, who was a bridesmaid. They had promised their elders there would be no larks or giggling and, as it turned out, they both behaved admirably.

As the years went by, Edward always did well on auspicious occasions. The royal training coupled with the seeds of showmanship which would emerge later, made a good partnership.

In 1977 came his mother's Silver Jubilee, chiefly remembered by the thirteen-year-old for the sensational fireworks display which he watched with his cousins and other members of the family. The timely lesson of his brother Andrew's hangover after too many celebration drinks, was not forgotten either. Significantly Andrew has hardly touched a drop since and Edward is not particularly interested; he will have a social drink with his friends but not many.

Heatherdown had found Edward an easier pupil than Andrew who, even then, could be pompous, moody and clearly conscious of his royal rank. Edward's nature was more like his eldest brother Charles', although he tended to be more outgoing, 'not nearly so shy', said one of his cousins.

As the years went by, Edward always did well on auspicious occasions. His royal training coupled with his flair for theatre, made a good partnership.

But his royal background was sharply accentuated when he was asked to draw a house at Gibbs. Everyone else in the class came up with the normal-sized, everyday kind of house most of them lived in – certainly in London. Edward's was rather different – quite clearly a palace with sentries outside.

The emergence of royal children into normal school lives has had its share of problems. By far the most difficult has been the question of privacy for vulnerable youngsters of such tender years.

'You cannot have it both ways,' said the Duke of Edinburgh in a television interview. 'We try to keep the children out of the public eye so that they can grow up as normal as possible. But if you are going to have a monarchy you have got to have a family and the family's got to be in the public eye.'

At Gordonstoun Edward was a popular and conscientious pupil. He didn't throw his weight about like Andrew and, although not as showily successful with the girl pupils, made some friendships which still endure today. Prince Philip had taught all three boys to sail, and Edward continued to do so at Gordonstoun, conveniently situated on the Moray Firth. Like his brothers he also learnt to fly at school as a member of the Air Training Corps. After two days training at RAF Benson he flew solo on the third day.

Because his teeth had to be straightened by a brace during his teenage years, Edward was known, inevitably, as 'Jaws' at Gordonstoun. His other nickname, used mainly by his cousins, is 'Earl', following their practice of using initials. In the inner family circle he is known as 'Eddie'.

He was seventeen when he had a junior starring role in a major royal production. It was Prince Charles's wedding to Lady Diana Spencer, and his two brothers acted as 'supporters'. They stood beside the Prince of Wales in St Paul's Cathedral at the start of the ceremony. Afterwards at the wedding reception for family and close friends, they announced each guest by waving rattles, and amusing the Queen and her guests by describing them in an unorthodox fashion: 'One King in Exile' was King Constantine 'Tino' of Greece; 'One King of Norway' was 'Uncle' Olaf, and many more of the British and European royals linked by their common ancestry with Queen Victoria and the Danish Royal Family.

Like many another, Edward was smitten with his new sister-in-law and for a while his girlfriends tended to be Diana look-alikes. But he suffered from the same problem his brothers had experienced; a lack of privacy in his relationships. 'You become conscious of the feeling that if you try to get to know anybody they are going to suffer for the rest of their lives,' he said once.

He has a nice sense of humour edged with realism. After the security scare in 1982 when the Queen was surprised by an intruder in her room at Buckingham Palace she was noticeably edgy and shaken. As writer Ann Morrow mentions in her biography *The Queen*, Edward tried to make light of the incident and 'cheer his mother up, saying that the security would become so intense around the Palace that if a member of the royal family was spotted outside – at Badminton or Windsor – the cry would go up that "one of them has got away".'

When the time came to leave Gordonstoun Edward came home with nine O Levels and three A Levels. He had also laid the foundation of his future theatrical career by taking the lead in two plays, *Black Comedy* by Peter Shaffer and *Hotel Paradiso* by Feydeau.

By now his striking blond hair had dimmed to mid-brown but his eyes, fringed by long lashes, were as Windsor blue as ever and, at over 6 feet, he was the tallest in the immediate family.

After Gordonstoun, following the practice of sending each of the Princes to a Commonwealth country to complete their education, Edward spent two terms as a junior master at the Collegiate School, Wanganui, New Zealand. It was one of several Commonwealth schools that have exchanged agreements with Gordonstoun. Prince Charles went to Geelong in Australia and Prince Andrew to Lakefield, Canada.

When it was announced Edward was going to Jesus College, Cambridge, it nearly provoked a student riot. Two hundred students signed a 'Go Home, Edward' petition. His academic record, they argued, did not justify a place in one of the university's most elite colleges. One of the organizers said, 'Most students here have A grades at A Level and those who haven't are usually admitted on the grounds of under-privilege. You can hardly say this of Prince Edward. We are simply objecting to the principle that privilege can get you into university.'

Buckingham Palace explained later that Edward had become an undergraduate through the Royal Marine University Cadets entry scheme. Like Prince Charles he studied Archaeology and Anthropology, 'Arch and Anth', thought by some students to be an 'easy ride'.

Edward arrived as a 'fresher' in October 1983, when he was nineteen, amid tight security. He was assigned to the modern Chapel Court – known as 'Millionaires Row' because the accommodation was rather better than the rest of college – with his detective Derek Griffin.

'An ordinary young man at an ordinary university college,' said the Master of Jesus, Sir Alan Cotterall. It was quite an understatement, thought most students at the time, but Edward himself defused the controversy by blending in reasonably quickly with student life.

Soon he found a real niche for himself in the university's Light Entertainment Society.

He appeared in several revues and directed and produced *The Tale of Toothache City*, designed to entertain mentally handicapped children. Edward was in his element. He drove the mini-bus, set up the stage, got the props organized and picked the cast. 'He really sniffed the grease-paint; got the bug in a big way,' said one of his friends.

In 1984 he produced the University Rag Week Review and showed some PR initiative by walking into the offices of the local paper, the *Cambridge Evening News*, and asking if they could find him a taxi with a roof strong enough for a couple to dance on it. During the rag procession a taxi duly appeared, driven by the Queen's youngest son with two students dancing on top.

In another student production he appeared astride the shoulders of his detective who was the 'legs' of a giant called Edward. 'That's a novel way to guard him,' commented the Queen.

The university became used to seeing the Prince around and he integrated himself totally into the day-by-day academic world. He was not afraid to make fun of himself, and 'brought the house down' with his impression of his brother Prince Charles. 'We asked for it again and again,' said a student.

Just before his twenty-first birthday he appeared as a drunk in the revue *Catch Me Foot* which raised more than £1,000 for charity. Then came the gesture which showed how completely the Prince had swept aside earlier criticism. On the eve of his birthday, students produced a massive cake and Edward, wearing a bowler hat, danced through the streets with others in the cast carrying their bithday presents to him.

Later the Queen threw a birthday ball at Windsor Castle for the coming of age of the royal quartet, Edward, Sarah, James and Helen. The paintings in the Waterloo Chamber were wreathed in flowers, and an enormous party of family and young guests danced until dawn. 'It was a marvellous night,' said Lady Elizabeth Anson who helped organize it. 'Edward had lots of lovely original ideas.'

Back at Cambridge, Edward's studies were punctuated by week-ends of tough training sessions for the Marines. With 85 pounds on his back he trekked over miles of rough territory and went on a five-weeks commando course at Lympstone, Devon, which included canoeing, rock-climbing and training marches. He even gave up rugger, which he loved, so that injuries would not stop him taking part in the courses. Peter Higgins, captain of the Jesus XV, said at the time, 'He dare not risk injury. He's keen to do well in the Marines.'

He had already gained a lower 2nd pass in Archaeology and Anthropology – marks which might have been better if he had not recently suffered from a bout of glandular fever before the exams – when he decided to change course, as Prince Charles did, and study History.

Edward left the university with a 2.2 degree in history and a reputation as a popular student who had contributed considerably to university life. 'He didn't put on any airs and graces as we'd feared and was really well-liked on his own merits,' said one student. His senior tutor said, 'He has been a delight to have about the place.'

Edward joined the Marines full time when he left Cambridge. He slept in a spartan barrack-room or under canvas and worked out with some of the toughest PE instructors in the world. There were nine-mile runs, with a back-pack weighing 20 pounds, often over swampy ground; rock climbing up thirty-foot cliffs, or boxing, at which his sergeant said he showed 'grit and determination'.

In the uniform of a Royal Marines Second Lieutenant he stood as 'supporter' at his brother Andrew's wedding to Sarah Ferguson in July 1986. It was the last time he would wear the uniform on a ceremonial occasion. On 13 January 1987, Buckingham Palace issued this statement: 'After much consideration H.R.H. Prince Edward has decided to resign from the Royal Marines.

Edward spent two terms as a junior master at the Collegiate School, Wanganui, New Zealand, where the Prince and Princess of Wales paid him a visit.

Prince Edward blended well into Cambridge student life. He took his washing to the laundrette, played a good game of rugger, and had a pint in the pub most evenings.

All his life Prince Edward has tried to live up to the standards the Duke of Edinburgh sets his sons. But he disappointed his father by leaving the Marines and taking a theatrical job.

Riding in Windsor Great Park is one of Prince Edward's ways of unwinding after a working week.

'An announcement about his future plans is not expected for some time.

'Prince Edward is leaving the Marines with great regret but has decided that he does not wish to make the service his long-term career.'

This bombshell burst on the Queen and her husband over the Christmas break at Windsor and Sandringham. It was not unnatural that the Duke, as Captain-General of the Royal Marines, was deeply displeased and, as is his way, did not hesitate to make his feelings clear.

Among the media criticism there were more thoughtful views that Prince Edward had shown considerable courage to stand up to his father. The Queen, who is the more conciliatory parent in family disagreements, finally broke up the row which had lasted some time, leaving Edward exhausted and distressed.

The situation was not helped by someone leaking a letter to the *Sun* newspaper from the Duke to the Commandant-General Sir Michael Wilkins, Royal Marines, in which he expressed his regret at Prince Edward leaving the service. The Duke was rightly furious and took the unusual step, for the Royal Family, of issuing legal proceedings for breach of copyright. The newspaper had to pay an undisclosed sum to one of the Duke's charities.

Now there dawned a year of uncertainty for Edward. After the relative freedom of university and service life, he was back to living at home with his parents, undecided about his future.

Halfway through the year came some good news. He met a sparky, attractive brunette, Georgia May, during Cowes Week and liked her so much he asked his mother if she could join the family cruise to Scotland on *Britannia*.

Georgia, then twenty-two, is the daughter of David May, the well-known Hampshire boat-builder. She has been close to the Prince ever since their first meeting at the Royal Yacht Squadron Ball, which was followed by an invitation by the Queen to spend the New Year festivities at Sandringham.

Meanwhile Edward did his best to assuage his father's wrath by taking on more work for the Duke's Award Scheme and other charities. Even so, his duties were still much lighter than the rest of the family and were certainly not stretching him as he needed. He plunged himself into the organization of an event which was to gather a still more unfriendly press but which turned out eventually to be an extremely worthwhile venture for charity.

Edward's version of the television game 'It's a Knockout' was a controversial production in which he persuaded the Duke and Duchess of York and the Princess Royal to join him in a series of undignified antics which critics complained 'cheapened' the monarchy.

Nevertheless Edward's efforts raised £1 million for charities nominated by the four royal participants and, as the Prince pointed out, gave enjoyment to a vast audience of television viewers.

But he earned himself more criticism by storming out of a press conference because the atmosphere, he said, was 'hostile'. 'I was tired and lacking in patience,' he explained afterwards. He also admitted he regretted giving the press 'the opportunity to get their knives into me.'

Edward had met Andrew Lloyd-Webber and his wife, Sarah Brightman, when they had been invited to the Queen's sixtieth birthday show at Windsor, which the Prince organized. He was subsequently guest at *Phantom of the Opera*, which he saw several times, and dined afterwards with the Lloyd-Webbers.

From these meetings came the job with the theatre company and a new concept of his working life for Prince Edward. He has told his colleagues in the company that the theatre is his career now. 'He's genuinely smitten and mucks in with the rest of us,' said one of them. There is no doubt he is a hard worker and is already earning the respect of his work-mates. The 'graft' he is applying to the job is even getting the approval of his father who still, in his innermost heart, remains sceptical about royals in commercial enterprises.

Talking about jobs for his sons, the Duke told writer Douglas Keay, 'What I don't think people appreciate is that there are not a great many options open. They could go into the church but any commercial or competitive activity is always criticized . . .' The Duke added, 'You can't have it both ways. In the end if you want to keep out of that sort of argument the only option is the services.'

His youngest son has courageously resigned from the service job he disliked, and found himself another option – in a profession which has fascinated him since Cambridge days. Stage props and 'bums on seats' (theatrical jargon for a full house), are now high on his list of priorities these days – not really so very different from the royal soap-opera back home.

Edward once remarked, rather unoriginally, that life could be likened to a stage production. 'I play my part,' he said, 'they play theirs.'

The theatrical royal showed a genuine talent for showmanship.

Below: *Prince Edward checking on costumes before the start of the Tournament.*

Prince Edward's version of 'It's a Knock-out' was a controversial production which he masterminded himself.

Below: *The proud producer on the set – before the sniping began.*

10

The Future

The younger working royals – apart from Sarah York, an established star – have emerged from the shadows of the throne to make their own splash of light in the spheres they have chosen. As the years go by the gap between the inner circle of the Royal Family and themselves may widen, but on present promise the personal bonds are too tightly drawn for this to happen.

The Queen makes a point of encouraging those in the outer circle to feel part of the family unit by keeping closely in touch with them and, where possible, inviting them to kindred occasions like Christmas and summer holidays at Balmoral.

The Prince and Princess of Wales, being closer in age, are even more involved with all of them. Whatever changes are ahead for the Royal Family of the future, the ring of cousins and all their varied talents will be as much a source of comfort and strength to Charles and Diana as their parents have been to the Queen.

As it will be for most families the unknown new century ahead will bring its problems. What changes will there be in the monarchy? How far will the escalating amount of publicity surrounding the royal family spiral upwards? How can it be controlled so that the largely sycophantic 'mush' of today is recycled into the sincere love and respect a good monarch deserves?

These are hyper-sensitive questions for the Queen's advisers, some of whom believe that the present soap-opera obsession with the Royal Family is nearing its peak.

Reaction to the birth of little Princess Beatrice of York produced frenetic activity on the part of newspapers who paid vast sums of money for balcony views of the hospital and details of the Duchess's labour. Even more interest centres on the Princess of Wales and her two small sons who, in the first year of the new century, will be eighteen and sixteen respectively. Their first cousin Beatrice will be twelve.

Royal Family unity so firmly established since Queen Victoria's day shows no signs of disruption. In fact the close rapport that exists between the Princess of Wales and her sister-in-law the Duchess of York should ensure that the Monarch's family of the future becomes even closer.

Because the two mothers are so friendly, William, Harry, Beatrice and any other children the Wales and York dynasties may have will grow up together as an extended family – something that will make the Queen extremely happy. She knows from experience

The Queen with some of the younger royals: the Prince and Princess of Wales, Prince Edward, Lady Sarah Armstrong-Jones and Viscount Linley.

how restricted life can be for royal children, especially in these security conscious days, if their family boundaries are limited to just two – as it was for herself and Princess Margaret.

William, Harry and Beatrice all share the experience of being media stars even before they were born. But, hopefully, their down-to-earth first cousins Peter, eleven, and Zara, eight, will be a steadying influence in keeping their feet firmly on the ground as they grow older.

These fair-haired children of the Princess Royal and Captain Mark Phillips were the Queen's first grandchildren and have been brought up in the sensible and casually affectionate way one would expect of their mother.

Both Peter and Zara are commoners, something the Queen is believed to regret. But her daughter has always firmly declined titles for her children, which leaves the curious anomaly of David Linley, the Queen's nephew, being born a Viscount whilst her oldest grandson has no title.

Regardless of this, young Peter Phillips is every inch his mother's son. Mature for his years, with the beautiful long eyelashes of his uncles – Charles, Andrew and Edward – he has also inherited Anne's unselfconscious regality.

'He is a proud boy – very confident on his white pony,' says Jayne Fincher who has photographed him many times. 'His regality is not arrogant but quite natural. He is aware of who he is and very wary of the press.'

His sister Zara has wayward, windswept blonde hair which, now she is growing up, she wears in a headband. 'Zara has lost all her puppy fat and is really growing up,' says Jayne. 'She is beginning to wear tailored clothes instead of jeans and has a much-loved Burberry handbag of which she seems very proud.'

Zara attends a local preparatory school in Minehampton, a mile from her home at Gatcombe Park, Gloucestershire.

Peter Phillips is at a Dorset preparatory school and will go on to his father's old school, Marlborough College, when he is thirteen.

Both children are very close to the Queen who sees a lot more of them than is realised. During the school holidays she often drives down to Gloucestershire to spend a few days at Gatcombe Park. There she enjoys the relaxed country life she so enjoys, with her grandchildren.

As with the Queen's and Prince Charles's generations, cousins will be important to the youngsters still in the nursery. William, the future King, and Harry the next senior royal Duke, will learn as they grow older – as their grandfather Prince Philip once remarked – that another family member may be the only person they can trust to talk over problems.

Only someone born royal can fully understand the inherent difficulties. When the future Edward VIII, later Duke of Windsor, was an infant it was said: 'From his childhood onward this boy will be surrounded by sycophants and flatterers by the score and will be taught to believe himself as of a superior creation.'

It is an ever-present danger in all generations of royals, though it sounds as if the careful upbringing in the Wales's nursery is producing thoroughly normal heirs to the throne although they have such diverse characters in their ancestry as George Washington and Ghengis Khan.

Above left: *Zara and her brother Peter have no titles. Their mother says: 'They are not royal. The Queen just happens to be their grandmother.'*

Above right: *Both Princess Anne's children are keen and already expert riders and look set to follow both their parents into competitive horsemanship.*

Zara, *blonde and attractive, is just as riveted by horses as the rest of the family. Behind her the Queen is no less intent.*

Harry is quieter and less boisterous than his elder brother William. But just as full of quick-silver energy and mischief.

A thoroughly normal small boy with an awesome destiny ahead. William will be the forty-fourth monarch to reign since that first William – The Conqueror.

The Wales boys are very different, says Jayne who was asked to photograph them for their father's fortieth birthday. 'William is extrovert, giggly and great fun. Not dominant but confident. Harry is very quiet, gentle and polite. But both have heaps of energy – darting backwards and forwards, in and out of the room.'

When these two reach their teens the older cousins – Snowdons, Kents, Ogilvys and their youngest uncle Edward – will be maturing into their thirties.

Each of them in varying degrees will always be in the royal spotlight. For the immediate family the scrutiny may become even more searching and intrusive.

The Prince of Wales, forty-year-old heir to the throne, is too sensitive and intelligent not to be concerned about the trend. He, after all, will have to gather up the pieces if the pendulum swings too far the other way.

Public affection for the Royal Family is deep-rooted, but ground can shift. Even the revered Queen Victoria had to endure booing from Republican-inclined crowds during her reign.

The Duke of Edinburgh who started the in-depth publicity sortie into his family in its early, harmless beginnings, by persuading the Queen to allow cameras into her family life with the BBC's compulsive viewing 'Royal Family', rightly fears where media attention is heading.

In the beginning, encouraged by great public interest, the Duke approved a certain amount of controlled exposure of his family. What he could never have forecast was how that interest would take off with the marriages of his two elder sons.

To a public weaned off 'Coronation Street' to the headier delights of 'Dallas', the continuing saga of the Royal Family provides even more glamorous entertainment. Most seasoned royal observers agree that the present obsession, particularly with 'Di' and 'Fergie' is verging on the unhealthy. 'A little more respect and decorum would not come amiss,' said one.

But the family unit, so cherished by the Queen, is firmly established, and all her young friends will surely form a double-tiered, supportive circle around Charles, Diana and their children in the twenty-first century – whatever may befall.

Above: *It's hard for a small boy to resist sticking out his tongue at such crowds of people below the Buckingham Palace balcony.*

Below: *Royal cousins who will form the back-up team for William when his time comes.*

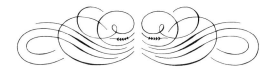

Bibliography

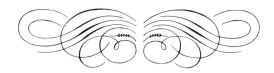

Beaton, Cecil *The Parting Years* (Weidenfeld & Nicolson, 1978)
Cathcart, Helen *The Duchess of Kent* (W. H. Allen, 1971)
Field, Leslie *The Queen's Jewels* (Weidenfeld & Nicolson, 1987)
Lacey, Robert *Majesty* (Hutchinson, 1978)
Longford, Elizabeth *Elizabeth II* (Weidenfeld & Nicolson, 1983)
Montagu-Smith, Patrick W. *Princess Margaret: Wife and Mother* (Pitkin Pictorials, 1961)
Morrow, Ann *The Queen* (Granada, 1984)
Plumb, J. H., and Wheldon, Huw *Royal Heritage* (BBC, 1977)
Roberts, Jane *Royal Artists* (Grafton, 1987)
Warwick, Christopher *Princess Margaret* (Weidenfeld & Nicolson, 1983)
Warwick, Christopher, and Garner, Valerie *The Duke and Duchess of York* (Sidgwick and Jackson, 1986)
Warwick, Christopher *George and Marina* (Weidenfeld & Nicolson, 1988)

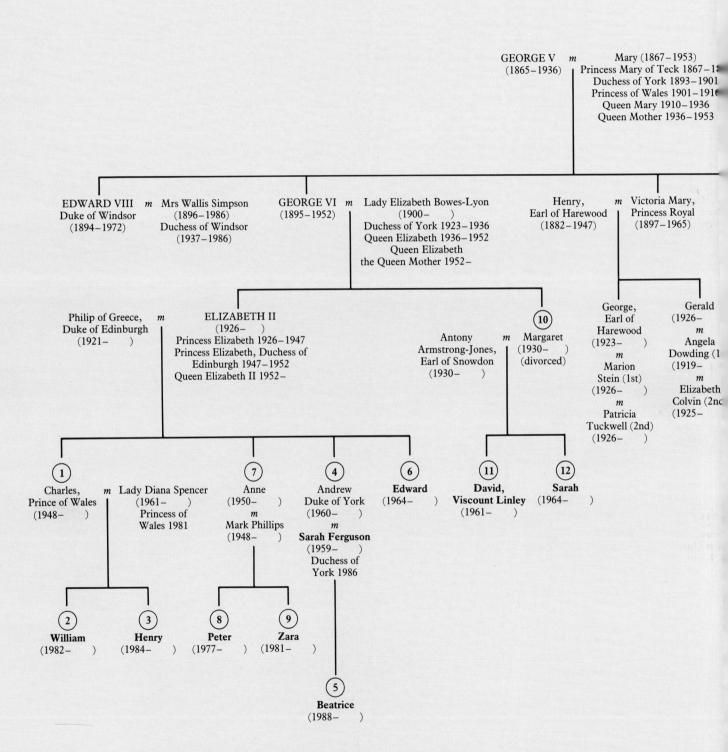

GEORGE V   *m*   Mary (1867–1953)
(1865–1936)   Princess Mary of Teck 1867–1͏
Duchess of York 1893–1901
Princess of Wales 1901–191͏
Queen Mary 1910–1936
Queen Mother 1936–1953

EDWARD VIII *m* Mrs Wallis Simpson   GEORGE VI *m* Lady Elizabeth Bowes-Lyon   Henry,   *m*   Victoria Mary,
Duke of Windsor   (1896–1986)   (1895–1952)   (1900–   )   Earl of Harewood   Princess Royal
(1894–1972)   Duchess of Windsor   Duchess of York 1923–1936   (1882–1947)   (1897–1965)
(1937–1986)   Queen Elizabeth 1936–1952
Queen Elizabeth
the Queen Mother 1952–

Philip of Greece,   *m*   ELIZABETH II   Antony   *m*   Margaret   George,   Gerald
Duke of Edinburgh   (1926–   )   Armstrong-Jones,   (1930–   )   Earl of   (1926–
(1921–   )   Princess Elizabeth 1926–1947   Earl of Snowdon   (divorced)   Harewood   *m*
Princess Elizabeth, Duchess of   (1930–   )   (1923–   )   Angela
Edinburgh 1947–1952   *m*   Dowding (1
Queen Elizabeth II 1952–   Marion   (1919–
Stein (1st)   *m*
(1926–   )   Elizabeth
m   Colvin (2n͏
Patricia   (1925–
Tuckwell (2nd)
(1926–   )

(1)   **(7)**   **(4)**   **(6)**   **(11)**   **(12)**

Charles,   *m*   Lady Diana Spencer   Anne   Andrew   **Edward**   **David,**   **Sarah**
Prince of Wales   (1961–   )   (1950–   )   Duke of York   (1964–   )   **Viscount Linley**   (1964–   )
(1948–   )   Princess of   *m*   (1960–   )   **(1961–   )**
Wales 1981   Mark Phillips   *m*
(1948–   )   **Sarah Ferguson**
(1959–   )
Duchess of
York 1986

(2)   **(3)**   **(8)**   **(9)**

William   **Henry**   **Peter**   **Zara**
(1982–   )   (1984–   )   (1977–   )   (1981–   )

(5)

Beatrice
(1988–   )